Get Down Off Your Horse !

By Tom Leftwich

ISBN   978-1-4583-8971-8

 LuLu Publisher ID 10158156

Printed in the United States of America.

INTRODUCTION: I have spent a wonderful lifetime enjoying some of the working experiences so vital to the development of western America. My Farm, Ranch, and Cowboy working years equipped me with experiences and skills that enhanced my horse racing and Rodeo skills. Later benefiting from Military duty and a lifetime of outdoor activities involving animals and gold mining, I lived some of the experiences of my ancestors. I have tried to capture the feelings of victory, defeat, fear, joy, anger and humor. I endeavored to describe these in fictionalized stories of ordeals in early Texas, Arizona and New Mexico Territories. I hope that you, the reader; get as much enjoyment from these tales as I did writing them.

Dedication

To the thousands of friends of mine that still enjoy our Western History and American values that built our great country; and to the Wisest Men ever Born in this Country, the originators and signers of the Declaration of Independence!

Table of Contents

Anderson's Regiment. A young man sick of murder and the mayhem of what these Terrorists were calling War, heads west hoping to get to California and start a new life. Immediately becomes involved in an Indian atrocity more heinous than any he had been involved in. Rescues a young woman in coma, two small kids and a broken legged Teamster. This action packed adventure involves the bitter hatred and fury of killing and the rescue of this young man from a career of wasted hatred!

Chapter 4   Get Down Off Your Horse

Young Jake Wins a Church Raffle and leaves home seeking the glamorous Western adventures of hero's he has grown up reading about! Reality crashes down on him and it is only due to the teachings of a Gun Fighter that his life is spared. Finally, realizing success in the job he dreamed of; he is met with a stunning demand from an Outlaw Killer saying, "Get Down Off Your Horse!" "Paco ! Kill him!"

Chapter 5   Keep an Eye Out for Indians !

An Ex-convict trying to escape false criminal charges rescues an old Apache Squaw dying in a freezing Teepee. Having found the Pablo Ortiz Mule Train Gold Convoy treasure just before his capture and imprisonment, he takes the old Squaw with him in his quest to recover these millions in gold bullion. An action and human interest adventure involving the use of a fancy Brougham Landau Coach .

Chapter 6   Stampede of the Gobblers!

A young married couple wiped out when their Business is destroyed by fire, attempts to herd two thousand turkeys From Hangtown ,California to Carson City, Nevada. This is a fictionalized version of the original turkey drive involving the eccentric nature of these birds and the many challenges facing a venture of this magnitude. Just when you think things are looking good, the birds are gone! Not one stinking gobbler left! Two thousand birds took flight! Everything we have ! Gone !   Quiet! Is that a gobbler, I hear?

GET DOWN OFF YOUR HORSE

CHAPTER 1

APACHE SQUAW GOLD

"Sheriff ! We want you to turn in your Badge!" Harsh and ungrateful words coming from the Town Council. He was Sheriff Austin Gray, of Sweetwater, Texas. Eighteen years, he had served this town as the Peace Keeper. Local crime and serious altercations had been low to non-existent up until two days ago, when he had become involved in a deadly shooting .

The Colin Bragg Gang had staged the holdup of the Del Rio Merchants Bank . Although they had come away empty handed; they had shot and killed two customers during the get away! One, was the young wife of the Bank owner. The Gang had split up heading north and the town of Sweetwater was right on their escape route. Sheriff Gray was in his office when three of the Gang rode into town and headed for the Buckhorn Saloon. It was his customary habit of walking the streets around ten o'clock and checking that everything was quiet. On this evening , he noted the three sweat stained horses at the saloon hitch rail and his years of experience warned him that something unusual had caused the hard use of these mounts. He also noted that the owners had not loosened the saddles as was a normal thing to do when your horse had been worked hard. This indicated the riders to be careless of their mounts or set for a fast exit of town. The brands were not from around Sweetwater and Gray thought , " Maybe I should see what kinda riders these were that would treat their horses this way!"

Walking into the Saloon, he checked his holstered Colt in a habit he had developed over the years. Maybe that was one of the reasons he was still around. Business was slow this evening with only a half dozen locals and three hard looking strangers. They were seated at a table sharing a bottle and Gray knew immediately that these were the riders he was looking for. He walked halfway down the bar to where he could see all three in the back mirror and asked Mike, the bartender for his usual. Mike handed him a short whiskey and he turned it in his left hand studying the three riders closely while appearing to examine his drink. All three were rough, bearded and a little louder than normal. Troublemakers was how he had them pegged.

One, a slender dark faced man; was probably a gunfighter . He had untied his holster when he sat down and this permitted his belt gun to hang normal for a quick draw. The one seated across the table from dark face was a big man with dirty blond long hair and he was wearing one of those long Walker Colts. The third man was a little older and some what quieter than his companions. Gray wasn't in a position to see if he was armed, but assumed that he was.

Having had his look and made a decision, he walked up behind dark face and asked the question, " You fellers ride far today? We've got a good Livery in town if you wanna give those horses a rest." The big man answered , " No, Mister Sheriff! They'll do just fine where they are . We stopped in for a drink and we'll dust outta your dirt bag of a town as soon as we finish this bottle! We don't need your concern for our horses!" Dark face laughed a little , but the quiet one said, "Take it easy Ed, the good Sheriff was just trying to be friendly."

Ed had taken on too much to drink and said, " I don't need no Damn Sheriff to tell me nothing!" Gray knew that things were beginning to get outta hand and said, " Calm down Mister, I wasn't trying to tell you anything. I consider myself a horseman and those horses could use a little attention! But ol' Willis down at the Livery is probably already in bed anyway and it's closing time for this Bar , so I guess you gents can head on up the road!"The big man jumped to his feet saying, " Are you telling me to get outta here ? I'll leave when I get Damned good and ready to go! I ain't gonna let some broken down old man of a Sheriff tell me what to do! You take your self outta here and find some old woman to give your horseman advise!"

The Bar turned deathly quiet! The locals turned around staring! No one in their recent memory had challenged Sheriff Gray like this ! "What would he do?" The big man spread his feet daring Gray to challenge him! The gunfighter turned half around and a nervous smile crossed the face of the quiet one! Gray looked straight on at the quiet man and said , "You either take him outta here peaceful or you and dark eyes here will carry him out!" The quiet man started to stand up and Gray said , "No! Stay in your chair! Once again! Do you take him out or do I ?"

There it was! Sheriff Gray had challenged all three in a showdown! Once again the quiet man said nothing, but let a nervous smile play across his face. The Gunfighter said; "Sheriff I think you're making a big mistake. We're in this together you know!" and he spun his finger in a circle! The big man , Ed had waited long enough! This was all the encouragement he needed! And with a loud "I ain't goin nowhere Damn you!", he grabbed for his gun!

Gray's draw was slow compared to the quiet man's who wore a shoulder holster and was lightening getting that gun out and triggering it in Gray's direction! Dark eyes, jumped up from his chair and immediately hit the floor! Grey's first round hit Big Ed before he could clear that ten inch Walker and he switched to the quiet man pumping two bullets into his chest. The gunfighter was out of it and all three were now laying on the floor! Three long seconds and three men down! Gun smoke was all that was left! Gray took a deep breath and shook his head. He had been lucky! Maybe there could've been a better way to handle this! He didn't know!

Looking at the gunfighter, Gray found that he had jumped up into the line of fire and caught two bullets in the back from his partner across the table! One was a killing shot in back of the head! He died instantly! Big Ed had taken the Sheriff's bullet near his left shirt pocket and probably died before hitting the floor. The quiet man was still alive, but sinking fast. Gray went to him and checked his wounds. One in the chest and the second high in the stomach. Mike , the Bartender brought some clean bar towels over for bandages, but there was little they could do for him. He would probably die within minutes. Gray asked him, "Mister, how come you to get in a gunfight? You could have easily took big Ed out and down the road!" The quiet man said, "Ed was drunk. Won't listen when drunk! Mistake , big mistake! Wiggins jumped! Sheriff , you knew, you knew, Smart!" He died!

Mike the Bartender. Asked, " What did he mean Sheriff , when he said that you knew? What did he mean by that? Did you know these men?" Sheriff Gray looked around and said, " What the hell are you talking about? This is the first time I've seen any of them!" Mike said, " Seems to me that he knew you and what's this big mistake he was talking about?" Gray said, " Look, it was a gunfight! He was talking about the gunfight Damn it! Some of you men give a hand! We'll get these bodies loaded in a wagon! Boot Hill can wait till morning , but we'll get'em outta here tonight!"Mike the Bartender, was not satisfied with Gray's explanation , but helped load the bodies . Gray took the three horses to the Livery Stable, unsaddled them and put them in with the rental stock. They would get a little feed and he would talk to Willis in the morning. Three men had died tonight and he figured he was lucky to still be alive!

A Posse arrived from Del Rio the following morning. Sheriff Jim Downing and members of his posse examined the bodies , identifying all three; as part of the Gang that attempted to rob their Bank. Del Hodges, the banker was with the posse and identified big Ed Blaken as the killer of his wife. He said, "I was hoping to be with the posse when these killers were caught. I wanted to see these murderers hang. Shooting was too good for them!" Sheriff Downing identified the gun fighter as Bob Wiggins , a fast gun from up around Dodge City and the third man was Colin Bragg, leader of this Gang of outlaws.

Downing said, " Gray you did the Territory a hell of a service taking this gang out of operation! These were some of the most dangerous killers in this part of the country. The outlaw Jensen and one other are still out there. If they come around, you may have some more shootin to do! I can't see how you managed to get all three at one time!" Gray said, " Jim , I just got lucky I guess!" Downing replied, " Yeah, lucky like a fox! I can see why this town has such low crime . A Sheriff with your experience and ability is hard to come by. Gray, we're going over to Austin for a few days and try to round up the other two killers. Should be back in ten days or so. The Posse is headed back to Del Rio, but I'll swing by and see how things are going. By the way, there's a Reward out for some of this Gang. I'll look into it while I'm at Head quarters." Gray said his "Thanks and Ride Safe".

Two days later, Gray is summonsed to meet with the Town Council and this is where he received that curt and surprising, "Sheriff! We want you to turn in your Badge!" Gray was dumfounded! He couldn't believe this was happening! Eighteen years and not even a Thank You from any of these dozen businessmen!

"Might I ask what brought this all about?" asked Gray.

George Bolton was the Council President and his reply was, " The killings that took place in the Saloon three nights ago were unwarranted in the opinion of witnesses and it's felt that a younger and more able man could have avoided gunplay. The Council has reviewed the account of all witnesses and we all agree that a new and younger Sheriff would be beneficial for Sweetwater. In all fairness to you, a vote of the members was taken and you lost! You will be paid through the end of the month. A young lawman from east Texas, Ringo Cauley has been offered and accepted the job!"

Gray was speechless! He finally managed to say, " All of you good folk's took a vote without even giving me a chance to reply and I lost! That's a joke! None of you voted to hire me! You begged me to take the job! Some of you remember Brown Lee? Yeah! The killer outlaw that was and still is terrorizing the state, but hasn't dared to set foot in this County since I ran him out! I should have killed him, maybe your Ringo will make him shiver in his boots! No, I don't want your pay till the end of the month! Here's your Badge!"

Gray threw the badge on the table , spun on his heels and walked out! Bitter anger, disappointment and a feeling of hopelessness followed him to his cottage on the edge of town. What would Margaret , his wife say? No job and fifty five years old! His savings were small! All had been spent for medical attention and medicine for his Margaret! She was doing fine now , but the three years of illness had cost him everything. He knew nothing else but lawman's work and wasn't physically able to work cattle again.

Margaret was upset and shocked by the actions of these folks he had served for so many years, but she was secretly pleased that Austin Gray would no longer have to risk his life . Maybe she could breath easy now when he walked out the door! She accepted what ever came to them without complaining. Gray was so thank full to have a solid woman behind him. This made it easier. He could expect her help rather than complaints! She volunteered to go to the Jail and help him pack up his belongings. By the time they had hitched up his team and wagon, he and Maggie ; as he called her; had decided on a plan of action.

They would immediately move to Austin and she would go to work in a Seamstress Shop owned by her sister, Gladys Hammer. She always wanted to do that and her sister was begging her to come. Gray looked at the belongings that they had and decided that two trips would be necessary. On their first trip. He would haul all of

Maggies keepsakes and look for a house in Austin. She could stay with her sister for a week or so till he had her sat up. After getting things settled in Austin, he would look for a job. Maggie dearly hoped that it wouldn't be in Law enforcement again!

Sheriff Downing was horrified to find out that Gray had been fired ! He demanded to speak to the Town Council and learned that the witnesses and their stories were nothing close to the truth. He straight out asked Mike the bartender to repeat his story and then , "Let me get this straight. You thought Gray was getting a drink to brace his courage? Did he drink it ? No ? I thought so! He didn't touch the thing! And he walked up behind the gunfighter Wiggins, taking him out of the gunfight and used him as a shield! That worked great! The big killer Ed Blaken took his bullet while Colin Bragg was shooting at him and hitting Wiggins. Cutting to Bragg who was momentarily stunned to realize that he had shot his partner Wiggins twice in the back; Gray shot Bragg a number of times .

This is one of the greatest pieces of Law Officer work that I've ever heard of and you people fired him hiring , Ringo Cauley from east Texas . Cauley is the Deputy Sheriff that was disgraced in Brownsville by a drunk Mexican. Cauley was so drunk he couldn't get his gun free of his suspenders! Cauley is worthless as a Lawman and is also a known alcoholic. By ten o'clock in the evening, he won't know a wet blanketed saddle horse from a camel! You folks deserve Cauley! You fired one of the best Lawman in the state of Texas! I'm going back to Austin to see him , I've got a Bank draft for him . It's $800 dollars Reward for Colin Bragg, the Outlaw!"

Days later , Downing caught up with Gray and gave him the Bank Draft. Downing was saying, " Gray, I know what it took in nerve and ability to take that Gang down! That was one hell of a good job! If you're interested , I can get you a position with the Texas Rangers. I know they'd take you on in a second!" Gray said, " No , Jim, I appreciate the offer , but Maggie is right! I had better look for something else! She thinks I've pushed my luck far enough. It's time to hang up my gun for hire and find something a little more peaceful! I don't have any plans right now and this reward money will sure come in handy. Thanks anyway and if I change my mind, I'll look you up!"

That evening , Gray went over his decision with Maggie and she was mighty relieved to hear that he was outta law enforcement for good. She knew that he was doing this for her peace of mind and not because he was afraid! Maggie was thinking, " I'm well aware that Austin was weaned on the smell of gunsmoke fighting outlaws and raiding Indians. He would not change overnight and become an armchair citizen. Give him a few days and he would come up with something to catch his interest. When he does , I'll get outta his way! That Reward money could be his start of something new."

Two weeks went by. Gray and Maggie were settled comfortably in a small house in town just a short walk from sister's Millinery Shop. Gray was getting a little bored with the usual Porch gossip at the local Grocery Store and wandered around town visiting with the Mexican families. One older man that he struck up a conversation with was Antonio Verdugo. Tony had lived in Austin for twelve years. Gray asked him, " Did you know a Carlos Verdugo that was killed by Brown Lee the outlaw?"

Tony angrily yelled, "Yes! Carlos was my brother! That murderer Brown Lee tortured and shot him years ago! He never did anything to Brown Lee or any of his Gang, but they robbed him over west of Sweetwater and killed him! I would give my life to kill Brown Lee!" Gray said, " I'm sorry Tony, I didn't know you were his brother. Carlos was at my home when he died. My wife and I had found him and tried to make him comfortable during his last hours. He had been shot twice and was in very bad condition . Once again , I'm sure sorry for your loss." Tony was still upset , but thanked Gray and wanted to personally thank Maggie for her aid to Carlos.

That evening, Gray ran over an idea that he had. He said, " Maggie, I ran into a Tony Verdugo today that was a brother to Carlos, that gun shot Mexican we picked up outta town a few years back. Remember, he had been tortured and shot by Brown Lee; the killer, and died that evening at our place!" Maggie said, " Yes Austin, I remember. You're surely not thinking of going after Brown Lee now!" "No Maggie. If Lee leaves me alone, I'll stay outta his way! Recalling Carlos though, has got my interest up! He said that he was carrying two California new mint gold coins dated 1862., when Brown Lee robbed him!

Those coins had to be part of that shipment of California gold meant for the Confederate Army and Lee tortured Carlos trying to find out where he found them. Carlos refused to tell him and Brown Lee shot him!" Maggie said, "Yes , I remember you talking to him about that. What are you thinking about doing? Going looking for lost treasure! That Cooks Canyon Massacre when the Apaches raided that California Confederate money wagon? "

Gray had been thinking of doing just that. He said, "Maggie , you know I have to find some way to earn some money. We can't make it on what you earn and this reward money won't last long. Carlos told me with his dying breath that the freight wagon carrying the Confederate Army gold was laying at the bottom of Cook's Canyon. It was empty, but he said that the front of the wagon was pointed in the wrong direction. He found the two coins on the uphill side of the road. He had an idea where the money box was, but died before he could tell me. Maggie that wagon was supposed to be carrying a million in those gold coins! I'm thinking of making a trip into Arizona with my wagon and try to find that treasure!"

"Austin!" Maggie exclaimed, " You know there's a thousand stories of lost treasure told around every camp fire in Texas! This could be a wild goose chase and you could lose what little money we do have!" Gray replied, " We got lucky with this reward money and maybe I'll get lucky with this treasure hunt. Anyway, I can't sit around here soaking up Porch gossip and you know the rest of that Bragg Gang is still running free and have sworn to kill me. I'll be safer out there where I don't have to be afraid someone is waiting for me to stick my head out of this house. A number of weeks away will help things to die down a little."

Maggie had to agree. It was common knowledge that he was living in Austin, but she still didn't like the idea of his leaving! Finally, she said, "Austin, I know you aren't happy here and I wish we could leave the state, but I know we don't have the money or a place to go. Maybe four weeks isn't too long and I'll be OK here with Gladys. You go ahead and look around over there , maybe you might find work in one of those Mining Camps." Gray said, " Maggie , you're one in a million! I have to find that treasure now , just for you!"

Word came to Austin that Brown Lee had raided the town of Sweetwater taking money and supplies from every merchant in town. He had attempted to rob the vault in the Country Store, but the owner was in Del Rio at the time. Four sticks of dynamite failed to bust it and two of Lee's gang were wounded in the effort. Brown Lee was angered when some of the citizens laughed at his efforts and burned the store down before leaving town. Every man in town was needed to help put out the fire.

Ringo Cauley, the new Sheriff, was no where to be found. Some folks reported that he had been seen headed north when Lee came in from the south. An Austin Deputy had been sent to tell Gray that Sweetwater was now looking for a Sheriff. Gray said, "You can tell them not to look my way! I've applied for a freighting job and don't want to disappoint the lady that is depending on me. I wish them luck!"

It seemed like he had been on the road for a month when Gray came in sight of the area where Cook's Canyon was supposed to be. He had been very close about letting anyone know where he was headed. The stores and bar rooms were his best source of information. As the canyon was in the direction of Tuscon, he asked for directions to the town and sure enough one of the helpful citizens directions sent him right through the middle of Cook's Canyon! Gray drove through without stopping and to any outward appearance was headed to Tucson. Circling a mile past, he turned off the road and doubled back to the top of a hill where he could camp unseen and visit the canyon on foot. He had brought glasses with him to closely study the whole area and try to figure out where to start looking. The hillside was steep and the roadway had a double switch back coming out of the canyon to the top of the hill. Gray decided to walk down and have a closer look.

There was no evidence of where the wagon had tumbled down from the road. The road through the canyon came out the west end and switched back to the left and in a full turn headed east along the rim of the canyon for a couple hundred yards to the east end. Here it turned abruptly to the right switching back and heading due west on top of the hill. Gray found the remains of the freight wagon on the south side of the canyon road . It was covered by low brush and totally obscured from the road way. Unless one had knowledge of it's existence, it would take plain luck to find it. He was thinking, "Carlos was right! The front of the wagon was pointing east! Part of the broken tongue and front axel were on the east end of the remains. Did the wagon spin around as it left the road causing it to tumble over and land in this manner or did Carlos find something else?"

Gray studied the wreck from end to end and climbed up the side of the canyon on foot following the probable tumbling fall of the wagon. If the wagon left the road above it's present resting place, there should be evidence of some of it's contents under the low growing brush. There was nothing! Gray was stumped! Maybe , Maggie was right ! He was on a wild goose chase.

He walked back up to his camp site. This wasn't going to be as easy as he had hoped. He tried to recall everything that Carlos had said. Over and over he repeated the conversation to himself, but no answer came to him . It was time to take the horses down to the creek for water. They had been on picket all day while he was searching the canyon. They were gone!! The horses were gone! Indians! Stolen by Indians! He had to get to his wagon and his rifle!

"Thank God!" he was thinking, " My wagon is OK! Nothing here has been touched! Indians would have ransacked it and set it on fire!" Gray was confused, "if not Indians then who would steal his horses and leave his wagon alone?" He had purposely parked in a small grove on top of the hill with clear ground all around, but anyone taking the horses would surely have spotted the wagon. He was trying to puzzle it out when he saw the boot prints in the loose dirt. That foot was a lot bigger than his! Horse thieves? "Could be", he was thinking, "but these two horses of his were just low grade Mustangs. Ok for pulling a wagon but not the best for riding or selling. People get hung for stealing horses and his two weren't worth hanging for. Something was not right , or had he been a Sheriff for too long maybe!

Getting out his Henry rifle, Gray checked the loading, grabbed a canteen and some jerky. He had decided to follow his horses for a ways! Whom ever had stolen the horses had pulled the picket pins and used the tether ropes to lead them off. Gray was beginning to form a suspicion and when he came upon tracks of shod horses, he knew that he was in trouble. The thieves had not even tried to hide their direction of travel.

Someone was trying to lure him into a trap or he was already in one! The tracks indicated there to be two riders and they walked their horses west toward a brush grove growing near a large wash out ditch. Gray would have to play their game for a ways. If he took off running , the thieves would run him down on horseback. He was in a wide open area and they could come on him at any minute! He was a sitting duck and had walked right into their trap.

Desperately he searched for some kind of cover that he might get to. Ever so slowly he drifted over toward that wash out ditch. If he could fool these killers for just a little bit , he had a chance! He squatted down a few times as if looking at hoof prints. It worked! He was less than twenty five yards from the ditch when the killers realized that he was on to them! They broke form the brush on horse back and started shooting at him! Gray high tailed it to the ditch and jumped in spinning around and opening up with his Henry! The killers were bearing down and within fifty feet when Gray's shooting knocked one from the saddle!

The other killer, spun his horse to the side when his partner went down, and tried to cut up the valley and get away. Gray had no trouble shooting him before he got outta range! He fell from his horse! Both killers were down! Gray went to the nearest man. He was dying, but managed to say, "Should leave alone , tried! , told Jensen, Too tough" these were his last words. Gray went to check on Jensen. He was dead! These were the last of the Colin Bragg Gang!

Gray knew that he had been darn lucky to figure out their trap and come away without getting shot! These killers ,had probably been following him from Austin waiting for a chance to kill him! He had a job now! He had to get rid of the bodies so they wouldn't draw more attention his way. Jensen's horse was handy so Gray mounted up and went to find his team. They were tethered beyond the grove of brush and he caught up the other horse, taking all four back to the wagon. Later , he found another wash out ditch two miles down the road to Tucson and dumped the two killers. His shovel came in handy covering up the remains. If the coyotes and buzzards didn't mind eating rattle snake killers, then here was a treat! Gray had no regrets for putting these two away! Maybe now, he could get back to his search for treasure!

Jensen and his partner had been packing food and ammunition and extra guns in their saddlebags. Gray went through their things and now he had an arsenal of guns. He also had two riding horses. There was no need to be concerned about brands! These had been blotted over till they were considered Mexican! Gray was thinking, "Staking out four horses every day and seeing to their care was taking a lot of his time away from his search for those gold coins! Dang! He remembered! Carlos had said that he found the coins on the upper side of the road above where the wagon lay! This was the clue! How does it fit? What does it mean? How did the coins get on the upper side of the roadway? Tomorrow he would ride over and take another look!" Gray was wrong! Tomorrow would bring another problem!

Morning brought a beautiful bright day to eastern Arizona Territory and Gray sat having his morning coffee. Suddenly he heard the sound of gun shots and running horses. A group of riders came out of the west at a high lope riding the switch backs down into the canyon and heading east. They seemed to be in high spirits, laughing and enjoying their early morning ride! Gray was concerned ! What had they been shooting at down on that creek bed west of him? That was near where he watered his horses! Catching up Jensen's horse, he saddled up and rode down to the creek.

" OH God! Indians!" He exclaimed to himself. Yes there were Indians all right , an old squaw and half a dozen kids, mostly young girls! These bastard cowboys had taken a lot of pleasure in shooting two burro's that she was using to haul her food and some of the little ones. It was true that Geronimo and Victorio's terrorizing in southern Arizona Territory had made the Indians fair game for anyone, but this was going too far for any fair minded person. We didn't make war on women and children. Gray was sickened by what these young cowboys considered sport!

The Indians were afraid of him. He tried to talk sign language to the squaw and finally convinced her that he wasn't gonna hurt them. He dismounted and picked up her packs tying them on his saddle. He indicated to her that she was to follow him and allow the little ones to ride his horse. Three of the smallest climbed aboard and he led them back up the hill to his wagon. He had plenty of flour and sugar. The old squaw had some kind of pulverized dry meat and ground seeds in her pack and mixed with that sweet flour , fed the kids a great meal.

Now Gray was thinking, "What do I do with them? I don't really want them with me while I search for treasure, but I can't just tell them to get out and go on down the road. The little ones will die out there without some kind of help! He was stuck! Weather he liked it or not, he had a family of Indians to take care of! Damn it !!" He made up his mind! The treasure hunt would have to wait until he could do something about the Indians.

Talking to the old Squaw in sign language , he told her he was going to butcher the burro's and bring the meat back for smoking. The Squaw was smoking a pipe of something that he choked on the smell of; but showed him a big toothless happy smile. Burro and mule meat was favored by the Indians over beef! Gray figured two carcasses would feed this bunch all summer. Three trips were necessary to haul all the meat back, but Squaw had started a fire and was ready to start smoking meat. Gray thought , " Damn , here's another problem. The smoke will bring visitors and he didn't need that!" Then he thought , "No, let it smoke and don't try to hide anything. Anyone coming by will think I'm crazy helping out Indians anyway! They'll make it easier to for me look around without being so secretive!"

The wagon made a great Teepee for the kids and the Squaw. They crawled in and out from under it and Gray threw his bedroll in the back. The accommodations weren't the greatest, but the kids didn't seem to mind at all. There wasn't a lot of time for hunting treasure and Gray still had no idea what he was gonna do about his Indians! Squaw was smoking dry horse manure or something that smelled worse and once again, Gray had to move outta choking distance!!

The old Squaw had scraped and dried the Burro hides as Gray had asked. He thought that with all these kids , he could use the hides to rig a travois for the Squaw when they left(whenever that was gonna be). He could let her have one of the saddle horses for traveling. Gray was beginning to enjoy the little kids and they were learning to speak English a lot faster than he was picking up Apache. They had been camping with him for four days and he hadn't had a chance to go hunting for treasure. One little girl of about seven was helpful around camp and took care of the two three year olds. There were two little boys and another girl of about five. Gray had no idea what their names were and got them mixed up most of the time.

The older girl "Natall", was playing with the other kids drawing in the dirt and showing the others how to draw a wagon when it dawned on Gray how the freight wagon may have tumbled to the bottom of the canyon with the tongue pointing east. Natall had at first had the tongue on one end and then decided to make the wagon go the other way. She erased the tongue and moved it to the other end! Gray looked at the road to the canyon and now!! He had it !! It was so simple why no one had found the answer!!

The freight wagon had been headed east on the upper road as it approached the canyon when the Indians attacked! It had gone off the road before it ever got to the first switch back! It had tumbled over rolling on to the lower road and continued rolling on down to the bottom of the canyon! That's why the tongue was facing east and nothing was ever found because the contents had been dumped out in that Manzanita brush between the upper and lower roads! Gray was so excited he couldn't hardly breath! He had the answer! It had to be ! There was a fortune laying on that hillside between those two roads! Carlos had found two of the coins on the upper side of that lower road!

Everything fit! He was gonna be a wealthy man! Gray couldn't wait! He had to get over there and see if he was right! He had saddled up and was about to leave when riders came loping into the east end of the canyon! Gray called to Squaw and pointed to the riders. They were the same group that killed her burros! She immediately shooed the kids under the wagon! The abject fear in her eyes brought a terrible anger to Gray! He hadn't realized how attached he was getting to his Indian family! Handing a rifle to Squaw, he pointed to the wagon bed indicating she should lay down inside.

The riders saw the smoke up where he was and came riding up the hill! Gray stepped out to meet them! The leader pulled up saying , " Hey Mister , what you doin here and what are you burning?" Gray could readily see that this man thought pretty highly of ,himself and he answered, " Well Mister what ever your name is, what ever I'm doin here is my business and I'm smoking the meat of two Burros that you and your brave cowboys killed a few days ,back!" The rider answered back angrily , " My name is Hooker and I own the Bar 6 Ranch ten miles out. You're on my grazing range and I don't like squatters! My Boys shot up an

Indian Camp a few days back and we'll do it again if they're around! You get your ragtag wagon outta here. That's the only warning you're gonna get!" Gray said, " Mister you're trying to cover way too much territory and before you get yourself in real trouble, I want to let all five of you know something. I'll kill the first one that makes a move for a gun! Every one of you are locked in with keepers on your guns! Mister Hooker you'll be first!" There was a deathly quiet that settled over the group! Hooker said , " Mister, we might be willing to take that chance! You can't get all of us!"

Gray said, "I can empty this gun before any one of you can get a gun out and I've got a sixteen shot Henry sitting right here! I hope you and your brave Indian fighting cowboys try it! That big Indian Camp you were so proud of shooting up had one old Squaw and six little kids in it! You brave Boys can be proud of killing the two burro's they needed for carrying a couple of three year olds! There's a rifle pointed at you from this wagon and any move will mean a dead cowboy! Now Mister Hooker, you ride forward and tell your cowboys to sit tight ! Any wrong move on their part and I'm gonna kill you!"

Hooker said, "Mister , you're buying more trouble than you can ever live with! I'll come back and even things with you , you can bet your life on it! OK Boys, do as he says. Our day will come!" Gray called , "Squaw!" and when she sat up with that other Henry rifle, every cowboy there thought their day had come all right! They expected a bullet any minute! Gray said , "Now Mister Hooker , I'm gonna give you that chance you want right now! My gun is still in my holster. Remove the keeper from yours if you like and we'll even things out right here!"

Hooker was looking at sure death! He didn't want any part of this gunfighter! Finally after Gray had given Hooker his chance to call or crawfish he said, " Get down off your horse! All of you! Get down off your horses!" They all dismounted . Gray drew his gun quickly firing two shots in the air! The horses stampeded heading down the road! He said , " Mister Hooker, I'm gonna leave you your guns. That's just in case you run into some real bad Indians on your way home! I do suggest that you stay plum clear of old Squaws and little kids! I'll make you all this promise, If I ever see any of you again, I'll shoot you on sight!" Gray didn't know how much effect his lesson in Indian courtesy would have on these cowboys , but he knew that they would think twice about following Hooker into anything! The loud angry complaining about a ten mile walk back to the Ranch started in earnest, but Gray sent them on down the road! He hoped to get outta there, before Hooker was able to recruit gun hands to come after him!

Gray was thinking, "I may have let my temper get a little outta control, but that Hooker bunch burned me the wrong way!" he indicated to Squaw that he was riding over to the roadway on the hill and that she was to keep the rifle handy for protection. She knew how to shoot and hopefully she wouldn't use it on him! Squaw was evidently happy, because she gave him that big toothless smile once again! She was firing up that stinking pipe as he rode away!

As Gray rode to the top of the canyon hill , he could easily visualize the Indians coming up the road past the switch back and attacking. They would have been totally hidden just past the brow of the hill and the drivers wouldn't know what hit them until it was too late! The canyon side bank was steep and the big wagon would not have stopped rolling as it hit the lower road! It would have rolled to the bottom where it now lay. In Gray's mind , the mystery was solved and now for the gold! Ground tying his horse, he climbed up the bank from the lower road and there laying buried under Manzanita brush was the broken remains of two wooden boxes! God! He couldn't breath! His heart was pounding in his ears! Pulling the broken planks and dead leaves off revealed, Piles of Gold Coins! He couldn't believe it! More gold than he had ever seen! Piles of the stuff! Two boxes of gold!! He pulled his gun! Was anybody watching him? This couldn't be real! No need for a gun, there was no one within miles! He had found it!! He and Maggie were rich!! God, she would be happy! God! He was happy! He filled his pockets with gold pieces. He had to take some out! The weight was pulling his pants down!

Gray sat down by the boxes. He had to catch his breath! This was beyond any expectation that he ever imagined! He had to calm down and start thinking. The boxes had been busted open by the Indians looking for food or ammunition. They had no use for gold! They had been disappointed! "White man collects soft heavy yellow metal; no good for weapon and no good for food, White Man Crazy!!" They had left it there! Gray was trying to figure out how he was gonna get it back to Austin! He had no containers or wooden boxes. He had a small keg for water on the wagon , but that wouldn't do. It wouldn't even carry half the coins! He took the saddle bags off his horse and started to fill those! He couldn't believe the weight! Half full and they weighed over a hundred pounds! Putting the bags on the horse, he returned to camp. There had to be a way!

As he rode into camp, the answer lay there on the ground above the wagon. The two burro hides! He could cut them in strips, fold them over and make long leather bags that would hold the coins. Thinking about it , " They would ride against the sides of the wagon all the way around. It would distribute the load and hide his fortune from the eyes of anyone." He tried to get Squaw to understand making bags out of the burro hides, but finally had to show her by making one. He unraveled one of his ropes to make stitching and in a very short time he had a long bag that would probably hold well over a hundred fifty pounds of coins. Squaw went to work making bags and Gray was starting to think about collecting his fortune and getting outta there! A big question took over his thinking, "What do I do about the Indians?"

That evening using his limited knowledge of Apache and sign language, he was able to learn from Squaw that all of the kids were orphans. Their families had all been killed in recent battles with the Union Calvary and they had no home to return to. She had been trying to get them all to the San Carlos Apache Reservation and Confinement Facility. This was the best she could do , but without her Burro's and food , she'd never get there with the little ones. They would die! Gray, looking at her and her age was thinking, " She is giving up her safety and risking her life for these little kids. She could very easily die on the road herself. I've got to collect this fortune and get it into a bank. I'll get it to Austin and then I can get her and the kids to the Reservation! They can travel with me!" Gray had made up his mind .

Squaw had built six long bags and Gray figured that they would more than hold all the coins. The following morning, he left the children with Squaw and her rifle. Driving the wagon to the lower road, he started collecting gold coins! It was late afternoon by the time he had collected everything from the two broken boxes. The wagon was loaded ! All of the Burro bags had been used! How much gold did he have? He had no idea! It was all tied up neatly laying completely around the side walls of the wagon box! Had he got every coin? Maybe not, but he had what he could find! There was probably some scattered down hill, but Gray figured that he had enough! Maybe one hour left of daylight ; It was time to head back to camp!

Suddenly! Rifle fire from camp! Two quick shots! He couldn't run the team up that hill, but he lost no time in getting there! Rolling into the camp area he was carrying his pistol in his hand and that Henry was close by his side! He was ready for a fight! Squaw had shot a rattlesnake! "Boy! What a relief!" he was thinking, " I'm getting too jumpy with all this gold . I've got to get outta here and get rid of this stuff!" His fears were calmed , but his concern turned to Squaw. She was skinning the snake to cook for dinner! Beyond that he was amazed to find that Squaw had shot two rattlesnakes! Both, through the head. Squaw could shoot! Gray was thinking later, " Well, I ain't much on rattlesnake meat. It kinda looks like fish and tastes like chicken! I think I'd rather have chicken! The kids loved it!"

Gray started packing his tools and camp together. Morning would be time enough to load the wagon. He let Squaw know that he would take them with him if they wished to go. Once again he was privileged to be rewarded with that big toothless grin! And once again he moved upwind of her pipe!

Morning! A beautiful sunrise in Arizona. Gray was thinking, " I'm sure gonna miss this desert country, but there's a bright future ahead for me and Maggie! I can finally give her the home she deserves. We could never have children and I'm sorry for that. It's the one dim light in their life. There was no family other than Gladys in Austin!" he loaded up his Indians and headed for Austin! Passing the hillside site of his discovery ; he wondered again at his good fortune. He was worried and anxious to get his wealth in a safe Bank!

North of his old town of Sweetwater, Gray was making good time, The Indian kids were doing great and although eating the smoked burro was getting a little tiresome; Gray didn't want to take the chance of spending any of those gold coins. No one paid him a lotta attention with that old

Squaw and a passel of kids. Squaw was happy driving the wagon when he rode out to try and find a little game. If he ate any more of that burro he was gonna start braying!

They were moving into wild pig country and although these pigs were small, they would make a change from Jackass! He shot two in a small glade about a mile from the road and although he smeared blood over the nose of his horse. He couldn't load it on his saddle. The horse went berserk any time he came near with a carcass! His final effort caused the horse to wheel away from him jerking the bridal reins loose and there it went running back to it's mate tied to the wagon! "Damn!," he thought, " now I've gotta carry the bloody things all the way back!"

Squaw saw him lose his horse, but there was nothing she could do but hold the wagon waiting for him to walk in. The ground was too rough for a wagon. Natall, got off and jumped on his horse bringing it to him. He was thinking , "Pretty darn good for a seven year old!" She indicated for him to hand her one of the pigs and the horse didn't object with her in the saddle. Gray walked back with her! He stunk like pig and was covered with blood! To top off his anger and discomfort, those Indians would not eat pig!! " Damn it!", He cursed, " They gobbled up rattlesnake like it was candy and won't touch descent food! Well the hell with it! They can eat Jackass! I'll eat pork!" Squaw wouldn't touch the pigs! Gray roasted a hind quarter and had to throw the rest away! Squaw didn't want it on the wagon! She didn't want him on the wagon either! Luckily they crossed a small creek where he could wash off the blood and some of the pig! He was shocked when Squaw threw Natall out in the middle. She didn't want her smelling like a pig either!

Gray would have liked to drive through Sweetwater and spend a coin to pick up some food, but once again , it might attract too much attention. Maybe he'd go hunting again! He drove around the town and headed for Austin. Just the thought of smoked burro killed his hunger! San Angelo was within a days ride, but by wagon, it would be almost two. They had a bank there and he thought they might drive through and unload all of his gold. He could buy all the groceries and beef that he wanted. He was thinking, " Fried chicken would be heaven! Maggie was a great cook! Austin was getting closer all the time!"He made up his mind. They would drive through San Angelo and deposit all of that gold! Get something descent to eat and get on down to Austin!

Gray drove in from the north side of town. Being the Sheriff that he had been for most of his life, he took note of things that most folks would ignore. There were a number of good looking well saddled horses standing at a hitch rail directly across from the Bank. Gray got that old feeling of pending danger. The hair on back of his neck was standing and the air felt suddenly thin for breathing! Something was about to happen and he needed to get his Indian kids outta there! Gun fire erupted from the Bank!! Slapping his horses he yelled, " Get outta here!" and spun the wagon around heading north! The left front wheel hit a soft spot as he turned and shattered collapsing! The sudden jolt and Gray was thrown from the wagon seat to the wooden sidewalk. Sharp stabbing pains in his side and arm almost blacked him out! The frightened horses continued to drag the wagon for a hundred feet or more with Squaw and the kids hanging on!

Men boiled outta the Bank shooting! The bank was being robbed! Gray came to his feet drawing his gun. The Bandits had made a break for their horses and were shooting at anyone on the street! Gray fired at one mounting with a moneybag! He fell to the ground and Gray hobbled across the street firing at another Bandit running toward the horses! Suddenly he was struck by a bullet in his right leg and was slammed to the ground. Brown Lee came running from the bank with a money bag and Gray brought up his Colt to finally kill this murdering outlaw. His gun clicked on empty!

"My God!" he thought, " Not now! " Gray couldn't reload , his left arm was useless! Trying desperately to pull the ejector with his teeth to open the cylinder and reload; he knew he'd never make it ! Brown Lee ran to his horse , mounted up and swung his gun over to kill Gray saying, " Good Bye Sheriff! See you in hell!"Suddenly from behind Gray, a gun blasted away, one, two, three times, blowing Brown Lee from the saddle! A wild look of horror and disbelief covered Lee's face, as he fell to the ground! Turning his head , Gray was met with the prettiest picture he would ever see! A big toothless grin from Squaw holding her Henry rifle!

Folk's came running from everywhere. A Doctor was called and Gray was carried by a group of willing citizens to his nearby Office . He was the man that stopped the bank robbery! Everyone in town wanted to help him. Gray asked that his Indians be taken care of. Many folk's , he found out later tried to provide for them , but Squaw wouldn't let anyone come near his wagon. No one in town was willing to go up against the lady that had killed the dangerous and infamous murdering outlaw Brown Lee! Gray had suffered broken ribs , a broken arm and a gaping wound in his right leg! Two days after the shooting , he was able to sign talk to Squaw and get her to accept repairs to his wagon and food for the kids. She preferred to stay in the wagon! It was noted that she did accept a good portion of tobacco for her pipe!

Gray was worried! The longer he stayed in town , the greater the risk for his gold being discovered! The local store keeper had been generous and provided him with a straw tick for the wagon bed and against the Doctor's wishes he asked to be loaded in the wagon. He and his Indians left San Angelo with Squaw driving! The bouncing was terrible treatment for his injuries, but as the miles rolled behind him ; to get home he tolerated and accepted the pain. That fragrant smell of good tobacco from Squaw's pipe was a welcome relief from burning horse manure!

Finally, the sight of Austin on the horizon and he was coming home! Maggie was horrified and distressed by his condition but came running and helped him from the wagon to a chair on the porch!. She looked questioningly at the Indians and was visibly upset by the dirt and filth on the kids and in the Wagon! Gray tried to explain, " Maggie this is an Indian family that I rescued and Squaw, here; saved my life! We need to get a place for them and food."

"Maggie! We're rich! I found the gold! You won't believe it!" Maggie in disbelief, said, " You don't mean it! You're funning me! Where is it? Where is the gold? You're not carrying anything!" Gray said , " Maggie look in the wagon!" She said, " Austin , you're light in the head! There's nothing here but blankets , camping stuff and rolled up grey hides of some kind! What are they

,bedding for the Indian kids?" Gray said, " Maggie get one of those grey hide rolls out for me!"

Maggie practically screamed when she tried to move one! Gray laughed saying, " Welcome to the rest of your life Mrs. Gray! That's Gold!" Maggie was speechless, "My God, Austin!" she said, "What are we gonna do with it! I never in my wildest dream thought you would find it! Is there really a million dollars here?" Gray said, " Maggie , I don't know , but it's more than we'll ever be able to spend. Mrs. Gray , you're in for a life of ease and retirement!" Gray looked to his Indians and Squaw had all the kids on the porch. Squaw still carried her Henry rifle and sat calmly smoking her pipe. Gray talked broken English and sign language to Squaw introducing Maggie as his wife . This was his home and Squaw and the kids were welcome! Squaw gave up her pipe long enough to give them both a big happy toothless smile!

Gray asked Maggie to walk down and bring one of the Sheriff's Deputies back so she would have an escort to the bank! He wanted to get that wagon of gold put in a Bank vault. The Sheriff Henry Franklin, came himself. He had heard the story of the San Angelo Bank Robbery and the death of Brown Lee. He personally wanted to meet the brave lady that killed the notorious Outlaw and to thank Austin Gray for stopping the robbery.

There was a $500 dollar Reward , but when he found out that Squaw was an Indian; he couldn't give her the award. Indians were not acceptable for consideration of Territorial Awards! Maggie and Gray were angered and Maggie said, " I'll sign my name to the award if that's what's necessary! I'll see that she gets every dime!" Sheriff Franklin was happy with this decision , he felt Squaw was fully deserving. Gray then told Franklin the whole story and asked for his help in getting the gold to the bank! Franklin was shocked and amazed when he saw the bags of gold coins. He insisted upon driving the wagon to the Bank with Maggie. Squaw was wanting to go also, but Gray asked her to stay with him and the children. He wasn't sure that she would be welcome in town! Indians were not looked upon kindly in Texas!

$733,420 dollars was deposited in Austin Gray's name. That was the amount that was rolled up in the Burro skin bags . One saddle bag laying in the wagon was forgotten and Gray decided to keep it and spend the coins as they needed. There would be a lot of buying over the next few weeks . His Indians needed to be taken care of . He and Maggie had made plans! Maggjie had said, "Austin ,I don't know how you feel about it, but these babies need a home, not some cold Teepee on a Reservation! We have a God sent opportunity to do something for them and Old

Squaw saved your life! What are you gonna do for her?"

Gray said, " Maggie I've had lots of time to think things out since I was hurt. Here's what I think we could do. Your folk's place in Tennessee was burned down during the War, but I know we could buy the land for taxes. I know how much you loved that place growing up. That's where we met and married! I want to move back to Tennessee, rebuild the old Plantation with a home that will house all of us. These kids need a home away from Indian prejudice and killing. We'll adopt the whole bunch including Squaw if she's willing!" Maggie said, "Austin, you've been reading my mind. I love these kids! They're wonderful! Let's go home to Tennessee!"

Weeks later, Gray went to visit Tony Verdugo and asked him if Carlos had a family. Tony said, "No, my brother never married! He was taking care of our Mother when he was killed! He loved her very much. It broke her heart! She lives with me now." Gray said, "Tony , I want to give you and your Mother something. It's a gift from Carlos , In His Memory!" He handed Tony a saddlebag with twenty five pounds of gold coins inside. Tony was speechless.

Gray left him in tears of gratitude and walked to the street where his new Covered Overland Wagon and four horse team waited. Maggie and his Indian Family were all anxiously waiting to start on their new adventure in Tennessee! Gray's new daughter Natall was going to proudly do the driving! (With his help!) Gray took his seat by Maggie and looking back through the wagon , there sat Squaw smoking her pipe with the other five of his kids. Squaw only left her beloved pipe long enough to give him her favorite big toothless smile!

THE END

Epilog: Twelve years later the Austin Gray family of Madison Tennessee, were celebrating the marriage of their beautiful daughter Natall. The plantation mansion was handsomely decorated and three beautiful Bridesmaids, looking like twins to their older sister; escorted Natall down the isle . Two handsome young brothers, stood strong and tall between their weeping Mom, Maggie and their white haired Grandmother Squaw. Austin Gray, the father; gave the bride away.

As Gray stepped back from the group, he hugged his weeping wife , noting that Squaw was showing her biggest toothless smile ever! "Damn!" He thought , " I went and bought her the very best set of handmade teeth that money could buy! She wouldn't wear 'em!!"

GET DOWN OFF YOUR HORSE

CHAPTER 2 Black Headed Billy

He came to looking up at a dirty dripping tent roof. He was laying on a bloody table sitting on a dirt floor. Jesus! there was part of somebody's leg laying in a pile of rags in the corner! The army boot was still on the foot of that leg! "My God!" , he was thinking , "They didn't even remove the boot before taking the leg!" "Oh My God !" he yelled, as realization came to him! "You Bastards!! You cut my leg off!! Damn you! Damn you!" he yelled, " I'll kill you both!!" Rolling over and off the table , he tried to stand up ! The pain in his leg swamped over him as he passed out! The two Medics picked him up and carefully lay him back on a nearby cot. They shook their heads , in understanding ; and moved to another table where another soldier lay in wounded torment.

Civil War medical attention was limited on the battlefield. The Medics had some little training, but there was nothing they could do for chest and stomach injuries. Operations were impossible and limbs were amputated when damaged beyond repair. Those soldiers with life ending injuries were comforted with pain killing laudanum drugs and laid out on cots to die. Amputees weren't treated much better. The soldier that had just lost his leg was identified as an enemy Confederate soldier, William Ballard. It appeared from his uniform that he had been an Officer wounded in the bloody skirmish fighting that had taken place the previous evening. That fight had been totally unnecessary as word of General Lee's surrender was just received that morning, and it was three days old!

Billy came to hours later , hoping that everything was a dream! Wrong! His loss of a leg was real and he lapsed into a feeling of despair and depression. Three years of fighting and leading his men into battle, watching them die or suffering the same fate as he was now seeing. There was never any satisfaction, there was no winning for anybody and now , for him ; it was over!. Twenty six years old and a cripple for the rest of his life! No home and no family to return to. Hell, he couldn't even ride a horse! Life for the feared Calvary Commander, Major William (Black Headed Billy) Ballard had just taken a turn for the very worse in Columbus, Georgia April 16, 1865. General Lee had officially surrendered the Northern Armies of Virginia to General Grant on 9 April, 1865. President Lincoln had been assassinated on 14 April. News of these events had not yet reached Columbus till after the battle! Billy, knew none of this and really wouldn't care when he did hear it. His life was now changed forever by his loss of a limb.

"Bad luck! Yea, he had sure got all of his during this last and useless battle. No prospects for anything and now he was gonna have to beg help until he could walk with a crutch!" These were Billy's thoughts as he lay in that dirty blood ridden cot. Looking around , though; he swallowed any self pity that he might be building. There were many with life changing injuries much worse than his; some from his own outfit ! Two more days and the Union Medics would be pulling out and moving north. The Union Army under the command of General Wilson like all of the Union Generals, reduced every fallen city like Columbus, to ashes! A terrible bitterness was felt by the whole southern population, because this battle occurred after Lee's Surrender and was regarded as unwarranted terrorism by General Wilson!

Once the Army had vacated , women from around Columbus came by the scores to try and comfort the wounded . Most of them had been victims of the destruction , but they volunteered their service and food for the fallen soldiers. Billy was ever grateful for the help he received. Most of his fellow wounded that had received medical attention from the Union Medic's were suffering infection. Internal injuries could not be attended at all. The women of Columbus were heroic in their efforts, but the horrid conditions of the tent facility could not be overcome due to the wanton destruction of the city and most of the soldiers died! Billy was one of the few lucky ones!

Days later Billy was moved to a small transport boat on the Chattahoochee River. Fortunately, this boat had come upriver after the city had been burned and was one of the few boats available to transport the wounded to better facilities down river near Thomasville. A former Rest Home had been converted into a Hospital Ward where some two hundred Confederate wounded were being treated. Many of those in the Ward were amputee's. Billy was just one of many and fortunately his leg healed without infection.

The amputation had taken the lower part of his right leg about six inches below his knee. A leather boot with a fitted oak leg was constructed to fit up to his knee and straps held it in place. His early attempts to use this peg leg were horrible. The pain was overwhelming and he elected to use crutches. The surgeons told him that he would have to keep working that peg leg or he would never walk again!

Billy took them at their word and spent hours of agony walking on a crutch with that peg leg taking more and more weight every day. A month had gone by and the pain was still severe, but he was able to hobble along using a cane. Every day he walked farther and farther forcing that right limb to carry his weight . The pain persisted ,but his use of the peg leg was almost natural. It was time to try riding a horse. His surgeon was very doubtful, insisting that travel by wagon would be more suitable. Billy agreed , but went for a ride anyway!

H e was in a hurry to get back home to Bedford Virginia and see his fiancée Helen Liege. It had been two long years and the letter exchange had been pretty bad. He had written a letter telling her of his injury, but so far ; no reply. The horse back ride proved to be much better than he anticipated. He was fully satisfied with his riding ability. A special stirrup was necessary, but he felt that he could easily travel all day without the pain he suffered walking.

Money was a problem. He, like most soldiers had none. His horse was lost to him and he was not fit for any hard labor. He applied for a one way freighter job driving to Mobile Alabama. The pay wasn't the greatest but Billy figured that there would be more opportunities in a bigger place to find work. He was right and for weeks he took these opportunity type jobs that no one else wanted and slowly made his way north. As he approached Virginia, he found devastation every where. The Union Commanders had burned everything. Crops were in the ground and beginning to grow , but people were hungry everywhere. Bitterness and pain would follow this terrible war for generations to come.

Finally getting into Bedford Virginia, he went to his own home place; only to find it burned to the ground. A small lean too shed near the pasture land was all that remained. His neighbor, Wilbur Stone; had cared for his place and his livestock, but he told Billy," The Union Army commandeered everything and burned what was left. Your Dad and I buried most of your belongings in the floor of the barn before the Union got here. Your Dad said the Deeds and most of the legal papers were in that trunk. I think that seeing the old place go up in flames just broke his heart. I wrote you about him dying. It just seemed like he gave up." Billie replied, " Yeah, Wilbur, I know you're right, loss of Mom and then this! He just gave up wanting to live! I really thank you for everything. I hope that I can repay you someday ! Right now I've gotta put some kind of life together. I'm still trying to adjust to being one legged! This afternoon, I'm gonna try and make it over to see Helen!" Wilbur held up his hand and said, " Billy, I'm sorry! I guess you ain't heard, she just got married last week!"

Billy was destroyed! This was the one thing that had kept him sane through the last three months. His faith in Helen and the certainty that she was waiting for his return to get married. He had to see her! He couldn't believe that she had given up on him! There had to be something else! He had to get over to the Liege Farm and see her! Loss of his Dad, loss of his leg, loss of his home and now loss of Helen! This just couldn't be happening to him!

It was a long mile and a half to the Liege place. A mile and a half that he used to run in ten or twelve minutes! Now , it cost him almost an hour of walking; trying to make certain that he didn't make any missteps that would bring on instant pain! John Liege met Billy at the door! It was obvious that he was not pleased. He very quickly said, "Helen is not here! I'm sure you know that she is married! She and her husband Paul are on their Honeymoon in Maryland! Why did you come over here?" Billy said, " I was not aware that she had changed her mind about our marriage and I wanted to hear it from her! I wrote her three months back telling her of my injury and letting her know my address and where I was. That it would be about six months before we could set up a wedding! I had no idea and it was a great shock to me that she wouldn't write me of her change in feelings. I expected a whole lot more openness and honesty from the Helen that I thought I knew!"

John angrily answered back, " What did you expect? You wrote that you had lost a leg, a cripple for life! There's no way you could work and support a wife! I told her as much! She'll be much happier with a whole man! Paul avoided the war and he will make her a good provider. He's going to join me in a bigger farming venture!" Billy got the message! His world was now completely empty and John Liege did not want any interference from him concerning Helen's marriage. He slowly and sadly walked back to Wilbur's place where he was much more welcome.

Wilbur and his wife, Maggie asked him to stay on with them until he could make some plans. Wilbur said, " Billy , I know Liege wants to lease all the farm land around here and grow tobacco. He has a great market available in Europe. His new son-in-law spent most of the War black marketing Tobacco to France and Spain. They're counting pretty heavy on getting your place. It's the best three hundred acres around here. The taxes are over due and I'll bet they're hoping to grab it at State Auction!" Billy said, " At auction it would go for a really good price, but if I remember correctly, it couldn't be in debt more than four hundred dollars or so! I know that Dad had a good bank account when he died!" " You're Right!" says Wilbur, " I remember he transferred it all to your name when we buried that trunk of his. I'll bet if we dug it up you'd find all of his accounts! You could easily cover those taxes and completely avoid an auction! Boy, that'll put a crimp in ol'Liege's plans!"

The following day , they uncovered the buried trunk along with a lot of keepsakes that belonged to Billy. The Account books were there all showing the National Bank and the American Savings Bank deposits. Accounts also shown outstanding notes collectable prior to the War. These notes were still in effect and owed to the Ballard Farm. By Billy's figures , he was not rich, but he wasn't hurtin either. He and Wilbur immediately drove into Bedford and transferred the Property Tax money . He also generated a Legal Proxy Note for Wilbur Stone giving him authority to handle the leasing of the Ballard Farm. He told Wilbur, "My whole life has turned upside down! I've decided to leave Bedford and head out West. I had other plans, but with no home or family, I just need to get away for a while and make it on my own somewhere else! If you'll handle the leasing for me , I'll split with you after expenses! I don't need that much money and it's the least I can do for you and Maggie!" Wilbur was shocked and surprised by Billy's plans, but readily accepted the generous agreement. This meant that he and Maggie would have a very satisfying income and could quit working his farm. He could lease it also!

They returned to Bedford the following morning and Billy started outfitting to head west. He had an idea that since he had been able to drive a team and freight wagon, that this was where he could find work. He purchased two riding horses and a wagon along with guns, ammunition , bedding and food supplies. He was down over a thousand dollars when he and Wilbur drove home, but he was also ready to leave Bedford! His dreams of trying to live in the old home place and raise a family with the girl he had longed to marry were gone forever . He swallowed his disappointment and headed west . He resolved to face head on, whatever came his way .Things couldn't get a whole lot worse!

Three weeks on the trail and Billy turned his wagon toward Santa Fe , New Mexico Territory. Wells Fargo had bought out the Butterfield Stage Line before the War and now with it over, they would be restoring the service through out Arizona Territory. This looked like a great opportunity for Billy to find a drivers job.

At the Santa Fe Office , he was informed that they needed drivers out of the Bisbee Stage Station. If he wanted a job , they would heir him on for the stage driver or a shot gun rider's position. The Indians were bad and every stage needed a shot gun rider for protection. Billy had never handled a four or six up team , so he elected to take the Shot gun job. His knowledge of guns and his experience in the War made him a natural for guard duty. The folks at Wells Fargo were concerned about his loss of a leg , but he informed them that it didn't bother his trigger finger in any way! His only problem was, he would have to get into Bisbee through some mighty lonesome and unfriendly territory where the Indians were active! He checked his guns and headed south!

The Desert Wells Road House was like a small Fort that sat just off the main Santa Fe Trail route. It was on the road to Bisbee and Billy planned on stopping there overnight. One more day and he would be close to Bisbee. He had counted himself lucky to make it this far without encountering any Indian trouble. Reports were out that Cochise and a number of his sub chiefs were raging all along the trail to Tucson! Most of the outlying ranchers had moved into the settlements for protection. It was just twilight when Billy drove into Desert Wells.

As he entered the narrow portal and adobe walls enclosing the compound, an older Mexican closed and locked the gate. Billy thanked him for letting him in and drove toward lights near a long low building. These were rooms where travelers could buy boarding for the night . Billy planned on sleeping in his rig and only needed to get feed for his horses. A row of desert brush cut his view of the porch way, but he could hear an argument going on between a man and a woman somewhere in that lighted area. Suddenly the woman screamed , " No! Don't touch me!" Billy jumped to the ground with his bad leg and almost passed out from the pain! He hobbled around the brush and confronted a big man holding a young woman by the hair and griping her arm! The young woman was struggling to free herself and the big man was laughing at her efforts. Billy interrupted loudly saying, " What goes on here?" The big man said , " None of your damn business Mister. Get outta here!"

Billy said , " It appears that the young lady doesn't want your attention! I suggest that you turn her loose!" The big man getting a good look at Billy, said, " Mister Cripple , you're sticking your nose into business that don't concern you. I'm Ruby Jacobs, the owner of Desert Wells and I paid for the lady to be here. Unless you want to lose the other leg, get the Hell outta here and leave us alone!" Ruby jerked his pistol out from his belt and started to swing it in Billy's direction! Billy had spent many long days looking for a way to expend his anger and frustration for the many recent misfortunes that had come his way. His anger exploded at the expense of Ruby Jacobs!

Billy's proficiency with firearms had been honed to perfection during the War and his pistol jumped into his hand! His first shot cut a neat hole in Ruby;s right arm and his second blew his left knee away. Ruby screamed dropping to the porch and Billy had to catch himself from firing a killing shot into Ruby's face! He stood there trembling at the almost overpowering desire to kill this man, knowing that he had purposely crippled the man for life! " My God!" he thought , "What kinda man have I become?"

The young lady was in shock at the quick turn of events , but almost afraid to come to Billy, and thank him! The terrible rage and anger was slow to leave Billy's face! Workers and guests came immediately to the porch area to see what was going on and the young lady explained that Mr. Jacobs had attempted to assault her and Billy had come to her rescue! Jacobs hired hands were apparently accustomed to their employer's animal characteristics with women and carried him inside to attend to his wounds. Billy knew that Jacobs would now suffer the same fate that he had. Maybe in the future , he would be a lot more tolerant of one legged folk's and maybe respect young women! Billy turned to the young lady and said, " I'm sorry Miss, but I guess I let my temper get away from me. The War was hell and things haven't gone too good since! My name is William Ballard , usually called Billy!"

The young lady introduced herself as Abby Winton from Bisbee saying, " I'm so sorry that you had to get into this. It's really my fault! I met Mr. Jacobs in Bisbee and he offered me this cleaning and desk job at the Road House. I just came in on the Stage today and it wasn't until tonight that I found out that he expected a lot more from me than my work. I absolutely refused his attentions and he became very angry and demanding. I don't have the money to get back to Bisbee and he advanced me the fare to get here. I know now that it was a dumb thing to do ,but he seemed so nice and Fatherly trying to help me." Billy said, " Miss Winton, you're very attractive but very naïve. There's a lot of depraved people in this world willing to take advantage of young girls. Where are your parents? How did you come to need this job way out here?"

Abby broke down crying! Billy apologized saying , " Look Abby, I'm sorry! I didn't mean to interfere. I'm going to Bisbee tomorrow, You can ride back with me . Have you got a place for the night?" Abby between sobs said, " Yes, Thank you, I'll meet you here in the morning!" She turned and ran into the entrance hall. Billy was confused by her actions , but put his horses up and crawled in his wagon bedroll for the night.

On the road to Bisbee the following morning, he learned the tragic story of Abby's life. In tearful and halting words , she had confessed a tale of horror! The previous October, her Dad's farm had been raided by the Apaches killing her Mom and Dad. She had been taken captive by the Indians and repeatedly beaten and raped before they even left the cabin! Two weeks , she had suffered at the hands of Apache Braves! Abby had endured despicable treatment! Billy was horrified and in tears of terrible anger after hearing of this atrocity. How could this young girl of eighteen, possibly keep her sanity after this kind of treatment?

Two weeks into her capture , Captain Carlton with a Detachment of Union Calvary routed the camp and rescued Abby. She said ," I was so thankful that I had been rescued and I willingly told of the terrible mistreatment that I had received. I later learned that this type of treatment was common for white captive women! I was asked by the Military to sign a statement which described in detail everything that had happened to me! This was a terrible mistake! Every family in Arizona Territory now knows that Abby Winton was raped by Apaches and no white man would consider letting his associates know that he had taken Apache left over's for a wife!

Every offer that I have had eventually involved demands to serve as a prostitute and I quit every job! That is why I took the Road House Job. It seemed like I could finally get out of Bisbee and go to work without the Apache issue. I was wrong!" Billy's anger was further fueled by this latest revelation and he almost wished that he had put a bullet in Jacob's face! Thinking back to that evening, he was still disturbed by the overpowering desire to kill that had come over him! Turning his thoughts back to the present, he noticed the trail was dropping down into a long narrow valley.

Billy did not like the confining hillsides. He was too much the Soldier. This place could easily serve for an ambush! He stopped the wagon and studied the roadway. Abby asked, " Mr. Ballard! What's wrong?" Billy replied, " I don't know that anything is ,but I don't like going into a blind valley like this! There is sign in the roadway of a group of unshod horses heading into this Valley! Do you know how to use a rifle?" Abby was scared!, " Oh My God!" she said , " Please don't let there be Indians!! Yes, I can shoot a rifle!"

Billy handed her his sixteen shot Henry saying, " Abby, I don't want to scare you ,but if I was an Indian looking to ambush a wagon , I'd hide out behind that rock formation over there and attack when the wagon rolled past." He pointed to a formation near the top of a small hill, about four hundred yards down the road.

Abby was terribly frightened and shaking at the prospect of another terrible capture! She steeled her feeling of panic, took a slow breath and said , "What do you want me to do? I'd rather die than be captured again!" she went on, "This rifle is different and I've only shot my Dad's hunting gun! He had me do all of the game shooting but it was a muzzle loader. I used it for killing squirrels!" Billy was impressed, "Knocking down grey squirrels with a muzzle loader! Wow! This girl could shoot!" He explained the rifle to her and showed her how to pump the lever reloading. He said, " I'd like to let you shoot some, but we don't have time for that! Hopefully there won't be an ambush and we can get on into Bisbee without any trouble.

If we are attacked though, here's what I want you to do. Kneel or lay down here behind these bundles and my bedroll. This will give you a good shooting position and I'll try to hold the wagon on the roadway as steady as possible. The wagon and your gun sights will be bouncing. The Indians will be horseback, so aim at the horses head and squeeze off your shots. You may kill a horse, but that's the middle of your target and a horse going down takes an Indian with him! Most of all, don't be afraid, DON'T BE AFRAID!, just take your time and squeeze off your shots just like you were shooting squirrels!"

Abby climbed into the back of the wagon taking a kneeling position as Billie had told her. Billy said, "That's good where you are! Just stay there until we get clear out of this valley! I'm going to drive slow until I get almost to the rocks and then we'll take off running. That'll give us a little more lead if we need it.

Don't start shooting until the Indians get within a hundred and fifty feet or so. I'll give the word! Are you ready?" Abby couldn't speak! She quickly bobbed her head up and down! Billy started the wagon down into the valley hoping that he was being overcautious. There was no sign of life anywhere. It seemed that all of the birds were gone even. It was too, too, quiet! Billy could feel the excitement and tension building up in him! Suddenly!! One of the horses perked an ear sideways and threw it's head up slightly. They were approaching the rock formation!

This was it !! He slapped the reins and yelled the horses into a breakaway run! Indians poured out from behind the rocks and the chase was on! Dust was boiling and Abby was hanging on for dear life. The Indians came off the hill in a rush. Some had rifles and started shooting at the wagon! Billy held the horses to the center of the trail as the Indians closed on them. His horses were fresh and giving those Indian ponies all they could handle. Billy had his pistol out knowing that

if they got close, he'd have to use it. Two of the
Indians were coming on fast and he yelled at
Abby, " Let'em have it!" Abby was laying out flat
in the wagon shooting over Billie's bedroll. The
bouncing around was too much trying to kneel!
Billy heard that Henry going! Abby was doing her
part! His horses were giving their best and Abby
was still shooting! Suddenly she stopped
shooting! "My God!", thought Billy, " Did she
get shot!" He spun around to look back and Abby
was still lined up aiming back over that tail gate.
He yelled, " What's the matter Abby? Why'd you
quit shootin! Are you outta shells?" She excitedly
yelled back, " No ! No!, We're outta Indians!!
They quit!'

Billy pulled the horses in and sure enough , the
Indians were gone! That is; what was left of them
were gone! There were bodies and dying horses
in the roadway a hundred yards back! Billy was
shocked to see the carnage that Abby had dealt
those Indians! Checking the Henry , she had four
shells left. He was thinking ,"I'll bet those Indians
thought they'd run into a Hornet's nest!" That
Abby could shoot all right! She had stopped their
attack and he hadn't fired a shot! He said , "
Abby, you sure aren't the same young woman that
I talked to this morning. That was the greatest
piece of rifle work I've seen from a wagon! Gal
you'll sure do to take along !" Abby said , " It
wasn't me ! It was this rifle! It never stops

shooting! Then savagely, saying, "Too bad they quit ! I'd love to shoot a few more!"

Billy then realized where that overpowering desire to kill came from! He said, " Abby, you just showed me why I wanted to kill Jacobs last night. That was my first opportunity to get revenge for the terrible losses and disappointments that I suffered. I almost killed the man! Here today, you've experienced the same feelings I had." Abby said, " I have never wanted to kill anything as badly as I wanted to kill more Indians! It's frightening. I'm still shaking!"Billy said, " You can relax. Looks like the excitement is over for the day. We'll reload that Henry and head on toward Bisbee. I know we won't see this raiding party again, but there could be other's down the road!"

Bisbee came in sight on the horizon and it looked like they would be in town about sundown. Billy asked Abby, " Do you have a place to stay for the night?"Abby said, " No , but I can probably get ol' Sam at the Livery to let me sleep in the hayloft. I've done that a couple of times already." Billy said, " It's OK for somebody like me, but surely not suitable for a young lady! I'll get you a room for the night and you can pay me back when you get a job." Abby tried to refuse, but Billy went to the rooming house and got her a room! He told her, " Tomorrow we're gonna see about getting you a decent job . I'll meet you for breakfast at that Country Café over there." Abby tried to thank him, but Billy quickly left the room!

Something was beginning to worry Billy , but he couldn't figure out what it was. He took his team to the livery pasture and rolled up in his wagon for the night., Tomorrow he would check in with the Wells Fargo Office and then see if he could find something decent for Abby. Thinking about everything that had happened that day, Billy came to realize that he was becoming more and more concerned about Abby's welfare. This was bothering him and he had his own problems to worry about.

Sunlight brought with it a beautiful day. It was gonna be hot, but that was normal for Bisbee. Billy met Abby at the café and Wow! What a beautiful young lady! He knew she was attractive, but this morning she was wearing a skirt and blouse that really grabbed his attention. How anyone could treat her badly was beyond his imagination. Even more so; how she could ward off an Indian attack was even more amazing! This was definitely not the Indian fighter of yesterday! Billy said, " Good Morning Abby; I can't believe my eyes, you are absolutely beautiful!" Abby , somewhat embarrassed said, " That's what a bath and brushing will do for a girl. Thanks for the room!" Billy said, "It was my pleasure and well worth it to have breakfast with a beautiful lady!"

Billy couldn't remember any day in the last five years when he had enjoyed himself as much as he did this morning. Abby was making him forget the horrors and disappointments of the last four months. He was reluctant to have it end, but he had to report in for that Stage Coach Shotgun job! He said, " Abby, I have to go check in at Wells Fargo and then maybe we'll go around and see if we can find you a job!" Abby said, " I've been to most of these places, but when they hear my name, the welcome smile changes to a "we'll get in touch if anything comes up!" I really need to move on to California where they've never heard of me, but I haven't the money to get there! I'll just have to keep looking!"

Billy didn't know what to say. He headed over to the Stage Line Office. Handing his letter from the Santa Fe Office to the Station Manager, it was obvious that he was disappointed! He introduced himself as Jim Thorn and told Billy, " We can use you OK , but right now I have no drivers. We haven't made a run to Tucson in over a week. The Indians are out and all of our drivers have quit. Mail has stacked up to about two hundred pounds. If you could drive a team, it would sure be a godsend! Right now I'm authorized to pay a hundred and fifty a week for a driver and the same for a shotgun!" Billy said, " I've driven a team , but not a four up! Give me a chance to drive one around and if I can handle it , why we're off to Tucson!" Jim was overjoyed with this possibility. If Billy could handle the four up , he could get a stage in route to Tucson.

The Station hands hooked up the team and Billy took it right through Tucson. He had a little trouble at first making turns , but the horses knew better and trained him. A half hour later and Billy was a rough four up driver! When could he leave? Billy said, " Right away" and then went back and asked Abby if she could grab her things and take a ride to Tucson. The job market there might be a lot better. Abby was ready and willing to go! Billy made arrangements with Sam at the Livery to see to his horses and with a small bag of overnight possible's, Billy was ready to leave! He would swing by for Abby at the Rooming House.

Jim Thorn had another problem! Now his Shotgun refused to go! It was too dangerous! He had been involved in attacks before and would find some other type of work! Jim Said, " Billy, I'm sorry, but we have no Shotgun for your trip. We'll have to cancel!" Billy said, " How about if I get my own Shot gun! Would you go along with that?" "Well yeah," Jim replied , " But this town is shy of folks willing to fight Indians!" Billy said, " I know just where I can get one that takes a real pleasure in killing Indians!" Jim said , " Great . bring him on! I'll hire him!"

Billy went to see Abby and told her he needed a Shot Gun Guard, but that she had to be a he! " A what ?" she said, " What are you talking about?" Billy said , " You are now Ab Winton, young Shotgun for the Wells Fargo Stage Line Company! Put on some pants, this shirt of mine, this ol'vest and rub some dirt on your face, Your hair will be OK if you don't comb it. This old Confederate hat of mine will make you look just like a young scoundrel. I'll get outta here while you change and don't look beautiful if you can help it!"

Ten minutes later and Abby looked like a low life Ab! Billy told her to mumble her words and keep them low when she talked to Jim. Jim was well pleased. He was skeptical of this young lad that Billy had dug up as a Shotgun , but that was Billy's problem. If he felt safe with this excuse for a Shotgun, then so be it! He was happy and pleased to finally get the mail going so his job would be safe. The four up stage rolled out at two o'clock that afternoon! Two hundred pounds of mail was on it's way to California!

Once clear of Bisbee, Billy said, " Well Shotgun , it looks like you have a job! And maybe I didn't tell you ,but it pays a hundred and fifty a week!" Abby was shocked, and said, " But Billy, I'm no Shot gun guard and as soon as they find out that I'm a girl they'll fire both of us!" Billy said , " Sure , they might ; but right now we're gonna run this mail through Indian Country and we're the only ones willing to do it! What have we got to lose. We'll pick up some wages in the meantime! I don't want to see you risking your life out here, but we're getting a little short on money. A couple of these high paying trips and you'll have the money you need to get to California. That Henry rifle, by the way is yours. Mine is in the Stage Boot over by me. I also picked up a pistol and gun belt for you. We're armed pretty good, but still have to be ever alert for an ambush! As soon as we have a chance , I'll show you how to use that pistol!" Abby was not looking forward to the day when she would have to leave for California.

Billy sometimes forgot that he had a missing leg. He had been reminded on a number of occasions when fast movement was necessary and he had taken a tumble, but it was becoming more natural for him all the time. Scrambling up and down into the stage was a problem and he really needed to modify the steps on the coach if he was gonna keep this job. Frequently his peg leg went through the steps causing him difficulty.

There were only four Swing Stations between Bisbee and Tucson, at this time; and Billy had been warned to keep the horses at nothing greater than a fast trot. This would give him rested horses in the event he was attacked by Indians. Coming into the Gila Tanks Station, Billy noted that something was wrong! There were no station hands about to harness up and the place was too quiet. He pulled up by the horse corral and told Abby," Stay up here, but get down in the boot and keep your eyes peeled. There's something not right about this station!"

Billy stepped down from the coach and Indians came out everywhere! Abby opened up with the Henry as Billy tried to scramble back up on top. They had to get outta there fast. Arrows were flying and some of the Indians had rifles. Billy was half way aboard when his peg leg went through the side step half way up and he couldn't jerk it loose! He yelled at Abby ,"Get the horses going! We've gotta get outta here!" Abby still squatting in the front boot, slapped the horses into a run going out past the corral and headed out into the desert. Billy was struggling with the straps to release his leg and finally managed to get free and up on top of the coach! Some Indians were chasing them on foot and he emptied his revolver in their direction. Sliding into the seat, he grabbed the reins from Abby and pulled the horses up stopping the coach.

Indians were moving toward them in the brush. Some had mounted their horses to chase the coach and Billy scrambled up outta the seat to a better fighting position . He spread eagled on top and with Abby in the boot, they opened up with two Henry rifles! Quickly, this cut the Indian's attack down to a standoff. Billy said, " Abby stay down and shoot anything that moves. I've got to turn this coach around so we can get to the road. Once around we'll make a run past the Station and head for Tucson. Trade me rifles, I've reloaded this one!"

Billy maneuvered the coach to a full turn and Abby shot at any Indian that moved out of concealment. They had been lucky. That Henry fire power was something these Indians had not experienced and there was no more threat of an attack! Billy made a fast run past the Station Corral and headed for the next Swing Station to get fresh horses. Abby climbed back up on the seat and Billy wrapped an arm around her. She was shaking and in a high state of nervousness. Billy said, "Abby, you did great! Just take it easy now and try to rest a little." Abby was thankful to have Billy's shoulder to lean on.

Willow Station was the last change before Tucson and both Billy and Abby needed a rest. Billy explained to Ted Garvy the Manager , that they had just survived two Indian attacks and would like to lay over for a couple of hours. Garvy said, " I'd like to help you out , but there's no extra room at this station. You can probably lay down in the coach for awhile." They piled up on two hundred pounds of mail and went to sleep.

Later, Billy apologized to Abby for the conditions and the rough language that the station hands were using. She said, "Billy ,don't worry about me . I've been called all those names. I understand that if I was dressed as a lady, these men would treat me as one. Don't get upset about it! It's not bothering me." Billy said, " Well it's damn sure bothering me! I won't have people talking to you like that!" Abby said, "Why Mr. Ballard, you're starting to sound like a Father or a husband!"

Billy was thinking, " You know something? That ain't a bad idea either! He sure was getting to like Abby's company!"Abby was thinking, "I hate the thought of leaving Billy and going to California, but staying here, people will talk about me and he'll fight ! I'll only make trouble for him! He'll be much better off without me to worry about!"

Billy was shocked! Abby was crying! He said, " Abby is something wrong? Did you get hurt in that last attack. What's the matter girl!" Abby catching herself said ,"OH No!, nothings wrong . I guess it's just nerve reaction. No , I didn't get hurt! How about you? That leg of yours must have got injured when you were trying to jerk it out of that metal step!" Billy said," Are you sure. You're OK. I get the feeling you're not telling me everything! No I didn't get the leg hurt! If I hadn't been in such a hurry, the peg would've come out easy. Now tell me what's bothering you?" Abby desperately said. " I don't want to go to California yet!"

Billy breathed a big sigh of relief. He didn't want her going either! "Look ," he said, " I know a hundred and fifty dollars isn't much! We can make a few more Stage runs until you think you have enough! They'll want us to make a return trip in two days! Are you Ok with that?" Abby said , "That'll work out great!" Billy noted though, that any mention of going to California brought a sadness to her voice. It wasn't something he looked forward to either!

The Tucson Manager, Tony Miller was thrilled that a stage had come through and he had eager hands waiting to transfer the two hundred pounds of mail. He told Billy, " I heard that you had Indian trouble, but you and your Shotgun fought'em off. This is the best news we've had in months. A few more trips like that and the Indians will leave us alone! We never have anything but mail anyway and none of them can read. Except for killing white men and stealing horses there really ain't much for them!"

Tony went to the desk and in checking the schedule, he asked, " Can you and Shotgun be ready to leave tomorrow morning? We have a special shipment going east and need to get it out right away?" Billy looked over at Abby and she shrugged her shoulders. Tony went on to say, " I should let you know that this trip will carry a heavy money box and fifty dollars extra for the Driver and Shotgun! What do you say?"

Billy looked at Abby and said , "With a good nights rest , we'll be ready to roll out at daybreak! We'll get a room for the night and see you in the morning!" Tony said , " OH No! , Billy , we have a room right here for you and Shotgun! Supper will be ready at six and we'll get you up at five for breakfast! Wells Fargo takes care of it's employees! There's hot water for a bath even! You'll find your bunks right in here!" With a "see you later" , he left Billy and Abby on their own!

Now here was a problem! Billy and Abby would have to share the same room and bath facilities. The out house was out back and private, but that bath tub was open to the room! Billy lit the fire for the hot water and told Abby, " I'm gonna sit outside while you get a bath and we've gotta be careful that no one suspects you're a girl! I had hoped to get you a room in town, but you see what happened !' Abby laughed at him, "Billy", she said, " I know you're trying to be a gentleman and very proper, but I trust you with my life! My privacy doesn't really matter that much. If I thought there was a threat, I've got my pistol!" Billy said," Damn it! I'm not worried about anybody else! I'm worried about me!" He went out slamming the door!

Abby just laughed , " She loved this man!"

Morning brought another hot day and early getaway for the Stage Coach. Abby was concerned about Billy and the fact that he had no hat since he'd given it to her. When she asked him about it , he replied, "I've got a thick layer of black hair on my head and I really don't need a hat. In the Army I had to wear that thing you're wearing, but right now it's doing a good job of keeping some beautiful features hidden! I really need a haircut. I'm not used to long hair, but for now it'll do!

By the way, we may be in for more trouble! Tony said there were four rough looking riders that headed east ahead of us! I think this strong box is loaded with gold , from it's weight ; and I'd bet somebody knows about it!" Abby says, " What do we do? If we're held up , do we just give it to them?" Billy says, " I wish it was that simple. No they would be just as likely to kill us to cover their identity and give them additional time for a getaway. They might not , but we don't know that! Our best bet is to try and be ready for them and get away if possible. Abby, I'm sorry that I got you into this . You could get hurt or killed!" Abby replied, " No Billy , I'm here because this is where I want to be. Whatever happens remember , I'm the shotgun and I'll do whatever you say!"

Billy reached over hugging her saying, "Abby, you're one girl in a million. I have never met anyone like you, but I don't want anything to happen to you. If we have any trouble at all, jump down in that front boot and open up with that Henry. Don't worry about me. I'll be rolling up on top and doing the same! OK?" Abby bobbed her head. She was scared for Billy, but didn't know what to say. She promised herself to do everything she could to help him. She checked her guns and set herself to be ready for anything!

They were a good twelve miles out of Tucson and approaching a long upward grade. Billy was trying to out guess the bandits , if there were any. In his mind the top of this grade would be the ideal place to do a Hold Up! The horses would be tired and the driver would stop to give them a rest. It was a perfect set up. Before he reached the crest, he had Abby get down in the boot telling her, "Abby, this might be the place. Come up shootin if it is!" As he slowly reached the crest, Billy pulled his Colt out ! There didn't appear to be anyone there. Just as he stopped the horses, riders came out of the brush on both sides of the road yelling for him to Hold Up!

Abby came up immediately firing and one of the Bandits went down . Bullets were flying and Billy felt a burn on his cheek , but he was too busy shooting to notice! Suddenly, My God! Abby went down !Blood was all over the side of her head. Billy went berserk! His revolver was empty and he grabbed the Henry , literally jumping off the coach to the ground and attacking the riders. He advanced on the remaining two bandits blowing them out of their saddles and continuing shooting until there was no movement left! All four of the robbers were dead!

Running back to the coach and scrambling up on top , he found Thank God! That Abby was up and alive! The ,bullet had caught her just above the left ear, cutting her scalp and knocking her down. Billy had blood all over his shirt front from a nick on his cheek and Abby was more concerned about that than her own wound. Patching each other up took a little while, but they made it into Willow Station without any more trouble. Reporting the attempted hold up, they changed horses and moved on eastward. Billy had all that he was gonna take.

There would be no more running the mail with Abby. She and he had almost been killed. Enough was enough! He would find another occupation that didn't risk Abby's life! He no longer thought of her as somebody else. She was part of him! Weather she liked it or not! He thought, " Would she Marry Him? Probably not! She would have this crazy idea that she would bring him trouble because of that Apache rape history! How could he get around that? He didn't know , but he had fallen in love with her and that was all that mattered to him!"

The Bisbee Stage Station was buzzing with the Apache Scouts report about the aborted attacks against the Wells Fargo Stage. Eight Apache Braves had been killed along with three horses! Raiding parties would now avoid a conflict with the Black Headed Warrior and his Shotgun. It appeared that Black Headed Billy was now feared on the Western Frontier! Billy didn't care about all the notoriety, he was done any way! No one knew it , but Abby deserved most of the credit for killing Indians; He had just driven the Stage! It was time to make new plans . Jim Thorne was not happy with Billy's decision and couldn't understand his unusual concern for his Shotgun. He finally determined that maybe Shotgun was his younger brother or nephew . He paid them their two hundred each and Billy and Abby went looking for a room. Abby insisted that they could share the same room and save a few dollars. Billy said , " No! I'll sleep in the wagon! Tomorrow I'm gonna straighten out a few things and we're gonna head for Tucson. I'll see you at the Café in the morning, but let's make it around ten o'clock. I have a few things to attend to first !"

It was another bright sunlight hot day! Once again , Billy met a beautiful Abby for breakfast and this time he lingered for an unusually long time over breakfast. Billy said , " Soon after we make a stop over on the Mexican side of town, I want to head for Tucson, so put all of your belongings in the wagon." Abby was thinking, " Well here it is. We'll get to Tucson and Billy will see me off to California. I shouldn't be sad! I'll get to where I can find a decent job and maybe start a new life." She couldn't stop the tears. It would be heart breaking to have to say Good Bye to Billy! Peg leg and all , She loved him!

Billy was aware of her tears, but this time he said nothing. His horses had been resting for days and he let them trot out a little. An old Pueblo Chapel was on the edge of town and Billy headed in that direction. Pulling into the yard , he helped Abby from the wagon and said, " I'd like you to go in here with me and listen to what this man has to say! He'll be asking you a number of questions and I want you to promise me that you will give him honest answers! Will you do that?" Abby, thinking that this had something to do with the Stage hold up, said , "Of course I'll do that Billy! I've never lied about anything!"

There were half a dozen people in the room and a man in a robe that met them looked like some kind of a Priest. Abby was shocked beyond belief when he said, "You are Abigail Winton and you are in love with this man, Billy Ballard?" Abby was speechless! The priest said , "Well?" She hesitated and finally said , "Yes!"

and then the Priest said , " And you Billy Ballard are you in love with Abigail Winton?" Billy answered quickly , " Yes!" The Priest then placed a white shawl around his neck and said, " We are gathered here to unite Billy Ballard and Abigail Winton in the holy state of matrimony!" Abby couldn't believe this ceremony. Was this real? Could this really be happening? Yes it was! Minutes later a marriage document was signed and Mr. and Mrs. Black Headed Billy Ballard were headed toward Tucson!

Abby was furious with Billy, "What did you think you were doing ? Why didn't you ask me first if I wanted to do this? Why did you think I would want to marry you? What kind of fool did you take me for?" Billy said , " Mrs. "Shotgun" Ballard , I love you and you answered all of your own questions when you said you'd marry me!" He put his arms around her, Abby didn't really object, and they headed for a honeymoon in Tucson!

THE END

Epilog: Fifteen years later, a proud Billie was watching his beautiful wife Abby, entertain dignitaries from Washington in the Ball room of the Ballard Colonial Home in Bedford Virginia. His two young sons and daughter were forever asking him, "Why do you always use the nick name "Shotgun" when you kiss Mom?"

And on a historical note: For decades following the Indian Wars in Arizona Territory, Wells Fargo Stage drivers wore their hair long and black in the custom of the feared Indian Fighter, Black Headed Billy Ballard!

GET DOWN OFF YOUR HORSE

CHAPTER 3

DESERTERS WILL BE SHOT !

"Deserter's of the Confederate Army will be Shot!" "My God!" he thought, "How many times have I heard that from Major Quantrill and then Captain Bloody Bill Anderson? Well, they won't be threatening me anymore! Bloody Bill is dead and so am I, Pvt. Socrates(Sock) Johnson of Putnam , Missouri, Deceased! That suicide charge across that bridge into the very mouth of three hundred Union Soldiers was crazy; just like everything else these two blood thirsty fools did! Bloody Bill was killed and I don't care where Major Quantrill is headed. Socrates Johnson has had enough! My identity now rests with the body of an unknown soldier killed in that fight at the Wooden Bridge following the Centralia Massacre and Railroad Robbery in Northern Missouri. No family and no home left to return to; I'm taking my horse, guns, and saddle bag booty and heading west! From here on out, I'll be known as Socrates Jones!"

The rider was a twenty four year old battle hardened young man that had experienced and participated in some of the very worst depraved terrorist raiding activities of the Confederacy! He had been part of the Quantrill Calvary Detachment

Charging through the streets of Lawrence Kansas killing every man and boy in sight and he had followed Bloody Bill Anderson throughout his murdering and killing sprees! His chance to escape from these groups had finally come at the Wooden Bridge Charge when he could place his identity on a dead soldier fitting his description. No, he wasn't innocent of crime, but he'd had all he could stomach ! His only excuse was " This is War!"Some how and some where down the road , he hoped those accusing eyes of men that he had killed would fade in memory and quit haunting his nightmares! Many times at night, he would awake in a cold sweat with gun in hand, to shoot his accusers! They were already dead!

Out of Missouri he took the Santa Fe Trail and headed into New Mexico Territory! Folk's were fleeing from Arizona and the Raiding Apaches under Cochise, The War had pulled all Union Army protection from Arizona and the Indians took this action to mean that they were winning! Under Cochise and a number of sub-chiefs, they had increased their efforts to drive out the white man. Hundreds of settlers had been murdered in Indian raids and hundreds of others had given up homesteads moving into Fort protected towns. More than Americans , the Indians hated Mexicans above all and constantly raided their Border Towns. The Mexicans reciprocated killing every Apache within gun range. No quarter was given on either side. It was into this pillaging and terrorist raiding activity that Socrates Jones was heading. Small bands of Warrior's recruited from the Reservations in Northern New Mexico and Arizona Territories were using any and all means of stopping Stage Coaches and Army Supply wagons to get horses, guns and ammunition! The Apaches had suffered raiding, treachery and abuse by the Union Army until any means of retaliation was justified in their minds.

Sock, had been involved in some depraved, and horrible experiences in his young life with Quantrill and Anderson, but fifty miles west of Sante Fe he came upon a new chapter in inhumanity! He had camped overnight in a little creek fed Valley known as Willow Draw just north of the main trail. He was in no hurry and his morning coffee was late in brewing. He had killed an Antelope the previous afternoon which he wanted to smoke the meat of, before moving on down the trail. It was approaching noon when suddenly the sharp crack of gun fire erupted from somewhere over the small hills to his west! Grabbing his saddle , he noted that the gunfire continued rapidly . There had to be an attack of some kind underway! Most likely Indians ! He checked the loads in his two saddle guns and grabbed his Henry rifle. Rapidly mounting, he spurred his horse into a wild run down the road and around the hill. Coming out of a grove of willows, he burst upon a scene of mayhem and murder!

A dozen or more Indians had attacked an Army supply wagon . Teamsters and Troopers lay dead or wounded on the ground surrounding the wagon. The Indians were stripping the wagon, killing and mutilating those still alive. Sock dropped his knotted reins around his saddle horn, grabbed out his two saddle guns and adopted the infamous Quantrill Raider's charge into this party of Indians! Riding hell bent down on them emitting his Rebel Yell, his withering gunfire was virtually unanswered by the Braves.

They were caught flat footed, having failed to reload their black powder guns. Indians were falling around him and some were getting away on horseback. His saddle guns were empty and he dropped them in his saddle bags drawing the Henry! The Indians were gone! Four were lying dead by the Wagon. Sock was thinking, "They'll never attack again!!" He had no idea how many he had injured, but the battle was over! At least for the moment! Only one of the Teamsters was still alive and Sock went to him.

The Teamster said, " God Man! I was sure glad to see you! I woulda been dead in two minutes! They killed everyone else , looks like! I got it in the leg! I think it's broke!" Sock said, " It' s broke alright, but not bleeding too bad. I'll get it wrapped up and here take my rifle. It's fully loaded! Just in case those redskins come back! Where were you heading when you were attacked?" Teamster said, " Well we were going to Fort Bowie ,but the Sergeant in charge changed orders and we detoured south to the Rio Alto Stage Station . I think he was wanting to see a lady friend that works there. Cost him his life!" Sock said, " How come you and the others to get out and leave the wagon? That seems like a dumb thing to do, especially in Indian country!" Teamster said, " Yeah, you're damn sure right there, but look over there!" he pointed to an open area near the road!

Sock couldn't believe his eyes. There laying in open ground was the bloodied body of a naked young woman and two small children, The kids were alive and sitting by the woman! Sock was horrified! He practically ran to the woman! She was alive! He picked her up and carried her back to the wagon. She had been beaten and deliberately knife cut in a number of places causing all the bleeding. Her feet and hands were tied! Sock was horrified, "My God", as he cut the ropes, saying, " What type of inhuman animals would do such a thing?"

Teamster answered saying, " It was a set up by the Apaches! A trap to get the wagon stopped! We should have known better, but when you come up on something like this , you don't think!

We stopped to help the woman and kids! Big mistake!" Sock said, " I've got to do something for this young woman! Will you be OK for a bit?" Teamster said, " Yeah, this leg is numb right now, but I should be fine for a little while. I'll try to keep an eye out for those murdering hyena's! There's a Medicine box under the Wagon seat!" Sock gave his attention to the wounds of the young woman. Puncture wounds in her stomach were his biggest concern. Luckily they were shallow and if he could control infection, she might live. He had seen a lot worse over the last couple of years!

The two little ones had followed him to the wagon. Their tears were dried, crying was over for them; they existed in a silent frightened state of shock ! These two little urchins had been part of a terrible atrocity, but fortunately for their own sanity; had no idea of the part they played in the murder of a teamster and five soldiers. He had interrupted the Indians sacking of the wagon , so most of the supplies were still intact. Two of the Trooper's horses had been killed in the fight, but the wagon four up team seemed to be OK. Sock tried to clean up the young woman's wounds, but the water keg had taken a hit and emptied. He needed to get her and the Teamster back to his campsite in Willow Draw. Gathering up all the guns and ammunition, he loaded the dead soldier's equipment on the wagon. Leave it, and someone would be in for more Indian trouble! The bodies would have to remain where they were. He had seen a lot of this before when hundreds of his fellow soldiers were left decaying on the Battle fields. There was nothing that he could do. His immediate concern would have to be for the survivors!

Laying the young woman in the wagon, he went to the Teamster and between the two of them , hobbled to the tailgate and got him in the wagon. The two little ones climbed the wheels and settled next to the woman. Checking around , he tied the horses to the wagon and turning headed back to his camp site. Sock was worried! Those Indians knew that he was only one man and that wagon was full of guns and ammunition! If they could reassemble and gain reinforcements; they would be back ! He had to try to set himself up to defend against a determined attack!

There was no way he could defend against twelve or fifteen Indians, he had to think of something else! There were fifty of the new Spencer rifles in the wagon and a couple thousand rounds of ammunition. He couldn't let these fall to the Indians! It would mean more raiding, terrorizing and killing of settlers. He decided to do something that would anger the Army, but might save a lot of lives. There were a dozen ten pound cans of black powder in the wagon and Sock was planning on blowing up the shipment. While he attended the wounds of the young woman, he planned a reception for the Indians; if they attacked!

He needed the wagon for transporting the two survivors and the kids. The Teamster was in severe pain , but bravely helping to calm the little ones while keeping an eye out for Indians. Sock had done what he could for the woman and covered her with a blanket.

He said to the Teamster, " I've got to move the wagon out about 200 feet and unload all that ammunition and guns. The Indians know it's here and I think they'll be back. I'm gonna blow it up so they don't get their hands on it! There's ammo and black powder. I'm gonna stack it together on the bottom and all the rest on top. It'll be in plain sight for the Indians! When it blows pieces of guns will fly everywhere. I'm hoping the Indians are nearby when she goes off! All I or you have to do is hit that pile on the bottom with one of those 44 slugs from the Henry. I hate to admit it ,but this will not be my first time blowing up a cache of guns to kill someone!"

Sock moved the wagon and unloaded the whole stock of weapons and ammo. He wadded a piece of white canvas around the Black powder cans so that it would be visible from his campsite. If the Indians came back that evening, he wanted a good target. Returning to camp , he spoke to the

Teamster, " Mister , I'm gonna try to put a splint on your leg! It's gonna hurt like Hell, but you can't let it go as is. It'll experience movement and far more pain if we don't do something. By the way, I'm Socrates Jones from Missouri, recently retired from the Confederate Army!" The Teamster knew better than to ask questions and said, " I'm Butch Herndon from Kansas. You sure were a God send coming down that road with guns blazing. I've never seen a prettier sight in my life! I sure want to Thank you ! You saved my bacon! This Damn leg hurts like Hell already. Do what you have to, I'll try to keep the screaming down! These two little kids have had all the frightening they need for a lifetime!"

The splinting and bandaging was tough and ol'Butch passed out from the pain; before Sock was finished. He turned his attention to the two little ones. They were Mexican! He finally put a name of Pico on the little boy of five and Maria on the little girl of three. Most of his Antelope meat was well smoked and the kids dug in eating. Sock figured that the young woman must be their Mom and hoped that she would come-to soon! The kids were happily eating and he turned the wagon to serve as a barrier to the blast when that pile of guns went off. He had determined that he was gonna blow it up regardless of weather the Indians showed or not. He wasn't gonna go down the road sitting on a bomb. He tethered the horses and grabbed a piece of smoked Antelope . "Not too bad!" he was thinking, " Maybe I can rest easy for a little bit!" He was Wrong!

Indians showed on the skyline! He grabbed his Henry rifle! Puffs of smoke were showing on a far hillside! Sock was not familiar with Indian activities and would have really been concerned had he known that a party of twenty were coming to join the remnants of those that attacked the wagon. He was worried, but Thank God ol' Butch came awake! Sock said, " Butch, I hope you're feeling better! Sorry I didn't have something to ease the pain! We may be in for more trouble though! I saw Indians on the skyline and smoke from over yonder" Butch said, " Yeah, that's bad medicine. That smoke means they're talkin alright! We better git ready for 'em!"

Seeing what Sock had done with the pile of guns, he said, " Mister Socrates, you've got a pretty good trap set up there, but you need to add one wrinkle to it! Go out there and take one of those rifles and stick it on top of the pile with a white rag tied to it. Some of these Indians have probably seen a surrender flag like that before and it'll draw them in close to your bomb!" Sock hurried to put up the flag and stacked boxes under the wagon to shoot from behind. He told Butch, " I'm gonna get you and the woman under the wagon with the kids. You'll have to guard our back door! We've got plenty of ammo and hopefully we can hold them off! If a few of them gather near the gun pile , I'll blow it up! After that , whatever happens; we'll give 'em Hell!"

Sundown and still no Indians! This was bad, they couldn't see the gun pile! The Indians could come and take as many as they pleased! Sock had to do something! Butch was chewing on Antelope when Sock said, " Butch , it's so dark I can't see a thing! I'm gonna move out to that mound by the creek and see if I can get a better look! I know the Indians are by that pile of guns! I can hear noise from over there! Keep your head down and keep those kids by your side. If I can see at all, I'm gonna blow it up!"

Minutes later , Sock had crawled to the mound and hunkered down on the creek side. He wasn't in the best of positions , but it would have to do. Very faintly he could make out the gun pile against the western horizon and he would have to fire almost blindly at the bottom hoping to ignite that black powder. He could make out horsemen moving near by . Maybe he could get a few Indians! He blindly fired at the mound One, two ,three times rapidly, then KaBoom! A double explosion lighting up the whole country side! Sock flattened himself down; almost in the creek! Shrapnel blew over his head and debris rained down all around him. Then total darkness! He heard sounds coming from the area of the explosion , but without light ; it was too risky to go over there! He would go back to the wagon and wait for daylight! Butch and the kids were OK!

Daylight and destruction! This sight met Sock at sunrise! Bodies of horses and Indians lay dust covered all around the explosion site! The ground , bushes and trees had been stripped of vegetation. There was no sign of the fifty Spencer rifles but hundreds of brass shells lay scattered around! His Wagon had suffered a few hits and more brass shells lay near . There was no sign of Indians anywhere. How many were killed? He had no idea, but some had survived and of these; he was concerned! He saddled his horse and leaving Butch with his rifle, he rode up the nearest hill to look over the country.

Far to the east he could see a dust cloud slowly moving away from his location. Hopefully it was Indians returning to wherever they were sorry they came from! Maybe , he, Butch and the family could get on the road to Ft. Bowie and medical attention! The young woman was still unconscious and Sock felt a deep sadness and anger for her. He had forced her to swallow a little water by the spoonful, maybe this; would help some. He didn't know! She had suffered horribly and would probably die! He had no means of helping her more than he had. He rein slapped the horses up a little, hoping to move along a little faster.

One more day and he passed through Apache Pass coming into Ft. Bowie in the early afternoon. He was not met with gratitude from the Fort Commander, Major Thomas; when he related their story and the destruction of all the rifles. The good Major said, " I'm sure that a good soldier would have died before he'd destroy government property that this Fort was solely in dire need of! Mister Jones, is it? I consider your action cowardly and pitiful! We desperately needed that load of ammunition!"

Sock responded, " Major , five of your good soldier's did just that! They died trying to save your guns! When I came on the scene those guns belonged to the Indians! I ran them off! I blew them up killing Indians ! As for your ammunition, there's hundreds of live rounds laying on the ground in Willow Draw. Send out a detachment and pick it up if you need it that bad! I need to see to a wounded teamster and young woman! Good day! Sir!!"

Butch was immediately received and taken to the sick ward. The young woman was taken by a medic to a surgeon's office . Pico and Maria wanted to go with Butch! Sock was surprised, thinking , "These kids should go with their Mom! I wonder why they want to follow Butch?"Some time later, a Medic asked him to come into the sick bay room. Butch was resting in bed with the two kids sitting next to him. He said, "Sock, how's the kids Mom doin? I sure hope she pulls through! These are two of the best little kids I've ever known! I'd sure hate to see them without a Mother!' Sock told him, " She's being examined by a surgeon right now and I'll get back to you as soon as I know anything. How's the leg?" Butch replied, " Medic says you did a good job. You should be a doctor! They changed the splint and put a good bandage on that bullet hole. I'll be down for awhile, but should recover thanks to you!" Sock was interrupted by the Surgeon coming in and asking him to step outside . The Surgeon didn't look too happy and Sock feared the news was bad!

The Surgeon said, "I'm sorry Mister Jones, but there's very little I can do for the girl. She has suffered a bad concussion. From her dehydrated condition ,I'd say, she's been in a coma for three days or more. I tube-fed her with a pint of salt protein solution, and I dressed all of her wounds, but I'm afraid without proper care , she'll die. You can't leave her here and I don't know of any place you could take her. I know it's a heartless thing to say, but considering her circumstances and what she's suffered already; killing her would be merciful! Sock was not prepared for this from a Doctor! He fairly exploded with, " Doctor! what the hell are you saying! Kill this young woman? I've never heard of such a thing! My God Man! What about her two kids out there?"

The Doctor said, " I'm sorry Mister Jones, but out here we have to be realistic about life and death. We treat those we can help and have to abandon the rest! I'm sorry! Oh! , and this girl is about eighteen years old, but she couldn't be a mother. She's never had a child!" Not the kids Mother? No hope for her? Sock was sick with despair! A beautiful young girl and she would die! No one to help her and no where to take her! Sock had been through a lot of hell and killing in his young life of twenty four years, but he sat and couldn't help crying in helpless pity for this young girl !

What could he do? What about the two little kids? What about Ol'Butch? He'd need some help too! Somehow , he'd have to help them all! He'd rescued them and saved their lives and like the Indians tradition. Their life was now his! He would have to make some plans! He went back to see the Surgeon and told him that he would be taking the girl to the wagon.

He had prepared a bed for her and another for Butch. He asked the Surgeon for a Tube feeder and what to feed the girl. The Surgeon said, " A meaty broth lightly salted would be best with plenty of water. She will choke on anything solid. When you use the tube ,be sure to insert it properly. She will be unable to swallow. This is not good ,but you can feed her a small amount slowly with difficulty. What is her name for my records." Sock said, " Doc, I don't know her name, you'll have to list her as a Jane Doe." The surgeon said, "Jane Doe it is , and she may come out of this coma at any time or she may wither and die. Also, remember she may not have much memory; particularly of the traumatic events that occurred just prior to the concussion. I wish that I could be of more help and I wish you the best of luck! You're sure gonna need it!"

Sock went to see Butch and update him on what was taking place. He related his talk to the surgeon and Major Thomas. Butch was surprised to learn that the kids were not Jane Doe's and wanted to know what Sock was gonna do with them. Sock said, " Butch, I have no idea. Their parents were most likely murdered by Apaches. I'll try to find a family to take them.'" Butch said, " Look no further, I and my wife Amy have no children. We'll give the little bits a good home! Our home is in Bisbee just south of here a few days ride. Amy will be thrilled to have these two!" Sock said , " Butch that'll be great! We'll head that way in the morning! Oh, and one other thing. Who owns this wagon and team? Does it belong to the Army?" Butch said , " No , it belongs to me. The team belonged to my dead partner and I'll have to settle with his family. Those two extra saddle horses belonged to the troopers that were killed. I guess they're yours, they're not carrying an Army brand!" Sock was feeling better, things were working out and now if he could get his Jane Doe to come around, everything would be great! She didn't!

Three days later, Sock had adopted a routine for feeding and cleaning Jane, the kids and Butch. This effort occupied a good part of his time and he was in a great hurry to get to Bisbee where help might be available for Jane. Butch was fairly able to tend himself , but Sock was the all around Nurse, Cook, and Mother for the whole bunch! The town of Bisbee was showing on the horizon when Sock's wagon was suddenly stopped by two unkempt bearded rough looking men on horseback!

Sock had seen them coming and he jumped to a high edge of temper when they demanded that he stop! Black Beard, the bigger of the two advised Sock that they were the keepers of this Toll Road he was traveling, and demanded two dollars toll for the wagon and horses. Sock said, " That fee appears awful high and I have not seen a Toll Road sign anywhere! I might consider a dollar if this is a Toll Road!" Black Beard swore and said, " Listen little man!" and pointing to his partner, " Maybe you don't know it but this is Rawley Benson the gun fighter and we own this road! We want two dollars for the wagon and now you can pay a dollar for each person on the wagon!"

Sock was not in a compromising mood! Frustration and fear for the possible death of Jane and the stress he had been under for the past few days had him in a very dangerous hair trigger state ! He sat still and just looked at Black Beard. He was trying his best to contain his temper! Finally as the time stretched out Black Beard convinced himself that Sock was afraid of him and rode closer to the wagon attempting to look under the sun blocking tarp that Sock had erected to keep the sun off Butch and Jane. Little Pico and Maria were seated by Butch and were scrambling back, frightened by Black Beard! As he reached to pull back the tarp Sock said, " Touch this Wagon and I'll kill you!"

Black Beard must have heard the threat of death in that warning , because he jerked his hand back ; like he'd touched something Hot! Unfortunately, his partner Rawley; mistook his move and went for his gun! Sock was no slouch with a pistol and almost welcomed this opportunity to fight some one! Butch said later, " Benson and Black Beard tangled with a Mama Sow Bear when they tried to push Sock Jones! I have never seen anyone as vicious and deadly in a gun fight! I thought that he was a fighter when he came to my rescue against the Indians, but that was mild compared to his fight from the wagon! He blew both from their saddles, although Black Beard never touched his gun and when they hit the ground, he was outta shells in his belt gun! He grabbed the Henry and pumped more bullets into both of them!"

Sock was horrified at himself! He couldn't believe the terrible anger and fiendish desire to kill that had come over him! He was sick with himself! How could he possibly be such a killer? He slowly walked out into the desert trying to calm himself as he reloaded his pistol. Ten or twelve bullets he had put into these two outlaws. They were shot to doll rags! He sat for a long time just looking at that beautiful blue sky over the hills south of Bisbee and tried to justify what he had just done! He couldn't!

Later , he removed the personals from Benson and Black Beard . Their bodies, he roped and drug from the roadway to a nearby ditch. He would turn in their things to the local law when he reported their death. It was time to get on down the road and into Bisbee before dark! Butch was anxious to see his wife , because she may have already heard of the Indian attack at Willow Draw and feared that he had been killed! He was also anxious to show Amy what he had brought her to raise and care for. The children she had wanted so badly! Sock tied the two loose saddle horses behind the wagon with his other two and slapped up the team into a ground eating trot. Bisbee was just ahead!

Amy was thrilled to see Butch and more so to be given the two tired little kids! She was overjoyed at the possibility that she could keep and raise them! Sock told her, " We've had a few rough days and I'm pretty sure the kids parents were killed by Apaches! These little guys have a reason to be tired. They're also tired of smoked Antelope!" He continued with, "Mrs. Herndon, I've got a young girl out in the wagon that's in a coma and I'll stay out there with her tonight. She's resting comfortably and tomorrow maybe I can find some help for her!" Amy was not too happy with that decision, but her house was pretty small and with the two kids they would be really crowded to add another bed. She said, "Mr. Jones , I can't thank you enough for bringing Butch home to me and I'll get some supper together for all of us in just a little bit!"

Sock thanked her and headed out to the wagon to check on Jane. He was frightened and appalled to find her thrashing about violently and making moaning noises! He placed a hand on her shoulder saying softly, " Jane, Jane , Please take it easy! You're Ok , you're safe easy girl, easy , don't hurt yourself!" She settled down still making soft moaning noises. He lit their lantern to see better how she was doing and was shocked to see her emancipated condition with her blankets kicked off! She had lost weight in the few days since finding her. He had not taken a really good look at her in the past few days as most or her wounds were healing well. Looking at her frail body, he knew that she was dying! A couple more days maybe and she would be gone! The sorrowful helpless dismay and depression that he had felt at Fort Bowie swamped over him and he broke down crying once again for the undeserved misfortune and suffering that was ending this young girl's life! He couldn't help himself in his weeping and when Amy came to ask him in for supper, he waved No and she understood! Amy thought possibly the young girl had died! He wouldn't be coming in.

Sock had hoped beyond anything that Jane would live and come out of her deep sleep. He had been talking to her every since he had cut the ropes from her hands. It made it easier for him to try and explain everything to her as he fed her and administered to her. He knew that her dying would not be something that he could have prevented ,but he blamed himself anyway! After all the terrible things that he had done , it should be him dying; not this innocent young girl! He swore to her, " I'll not give up on you! You will come awake ! I'll stay with you! I'll be here when you need me , I swear it!" He was sitting on the tailgate of the wagon weeping when he heard the most marvelous words that he would ever hear in his life! " Why are you crying? Who are you?" My god it was Jane! Sock spun around in shock and disbelief! She was alive ! Jane was awake! He couldn't believe it! " My God!" , he said, "You're awake!" Jane screamed! And angrily stated " Where are my clothes? Who are you? What am I doing here? Where am I ?" Amy came running from the house saying, "Mr. Jones ! Who screamed? What's going on?" Sock fairly shouted, " She's awake! Amy, Jane's awake! She's gonna live!" " Praise the Lord!," Amy said, "let me see her!" Jane was shaking in fear, but immediately moved toward Amy. Amy wrapped her in her arms trying to calm the young girl, telling her , " Darlin you'll be all right. You're safe. Here let me wrap this blanket around you. Sit here a minute and we'll go in the house."

Sock was still in shock! He couldn't believe what was happening! He was overjoyed with happy relief that Jane was gonna live, but she was afraid of him! He had seen the stark terror in her eyes looking at him! He was thinking, " What had I expected ? That she would immediately jump in his direction thanking him for saving her life! Hell, she didn't know him from Adam! She had been in a coma since he picked her up! He 'd have to try and remember that!" He said , "Amy, I'll go in the house and let Butch know what's going on! I know he'll be as happy as I am that Jane is awake! Do you think you'll need help with moving her?" Amy said, " No Sock, the poor thing doesn't weigh a mite! I could probably carry her! Go on in and see Butch! We'll be in as soon as she gets her bearings. Move those chairs around so she'll have a place to sit." Sock was glad to have something to do that would get him outta sight of those accusing eyes of Jane!

An hour had gone by, and Butch was getting worried for Amy. She and Jane had not yet come into the house! Sock went to check on them and here they came. Amy was practically carrying Jane! She was terribly weak and couldn't stand without support, but shrank back in fear when Sock offered to help her. Amy seated her and said, " Sock , bring that bedding in from the wagon. This young lady is staying in here tonight! She doesn't need to be anywhere that will frighten her. By the way her name is Emily Taylor and she's from a small place near Yuma. It's a long story. Tomorrow we'll talk about it . Tonight Emily needs food and rest."Sock went out immediately and brought in her bedding. Emily was seated by the table drinking a cup of supper coffee lased heavily with sugar. Amy was pulling out everything to feed her and Sock said, " Amy do you think she should eat that much right away? Might make her sick!" Amy said, " Lordy you're right! I wasn't thinking! I forgot you're her doctor!"

Sock noticed that Emily was beginning to feel a little easier with him and that fear was gone from her eyes. He said , " Miss Emily Taylor , I'd like to introduce myself. I'm Socrates Jones recently from Missouri and voluntarily retired from the Confederate Army. Please believe me when I say that meeting and talking to you is the most wonderful thing that has happened to me in the last five years! I am forever in your debt!" Emily only bobbed her head and went back to eating. She was still a little fearful of him! Sock figured that she might be afraid to answer his introduction. He had a million questions , but felt that those would have to wait until she felt more comfortable in answering them. He said, " Emily, do you wish to sit up for a while and talk, or would you rather rest? I'll stay up if you like!" She said , "I'd like to talk a bit Mr. Socrates, but I'm too tired. Amy told me part of my story and I guess that I shouldn't be sleepy, but tomorrow , I'll do better." Sock went to his wagon bed feeling better than he had for years!

Sunup brought a beautiful morning to Bisbee, but it also brought Sheriff Walt Guthrie with two Deputies to arrest Sock for the hold up and murder of Sam Barlow and Rawley Benson. He had been seen with their horses the previous evening and Barlow's brother Jake had investigated finding the bodies and notifying the Sheriff. Their personals were found in a tow sack by the wagon seat. Sock was in deep trouble unless he could produce creditable witnesses to clear himself! Would Butch's testimony be enough to clear him? He didn't know! After the great happiness of the previous evening , Sock was locked in Jail. Jake Barlow rode around town trying to get together a hanging party for Outlaw Killer Sock Jones! Barlow and Benson had not been too well liked and very few were interested in a hanging for their killer. Sock would have plenty of time to worry out his trial. The Circuit Judge would be two weeks getting to Bisbee . Socks problem became very critical when he found out that two witnesses were required to get his freedom.

Sheriff Guthrie wanted to believe him, but formal charges had been brought against him by local resident and businessman Jake Barlow. He was stuck. Two weeks before he could get a hearing and the evidence was not in his favor. Amy came to see him and kept him up to date on Emily's progress. She was coming along great and wanted to see him also. Sock said , " Amy, I can't thank you enough for what you're doing for her. I'm sure Butch has filled you in on her treatment by the Indians. Has she said anything about that?" Amy said, "Very little. She knows what you did for her and she wants to visit here as soon as she can. I've kept her from coming until she has her strength back. She's weak as a kitten and lost a lot of weight! Maybe tomorrow, I'll let her come along!"

The following morning , Emily shows up and Sheriff Guthrie was frightened and concerned by her condition. Sock thought she looked great, but then he'd seen her at her very worse! He said, " Emily you're looking wonderful. I can't tell you how wonderful it is to see you up and walking! Girl you've made everything I've done worthwhile! I can't ask for anything better!" Emily was embarrassed , but said, " Mr. Socrates, I'm sorry that I frightened you and was afraid of you when I woke up. I know now that I owe you my life! I don't know why you saved me when I should have died! Butch says that you are a very dangerous man! I can't believe that! You're the kindest person I've ever met. Why were you crying when I woke up?" It was time for Sock to be embarrassed! He said , "Emily,why don't we forget that! I was probably feeling bad or something! Grown men don't cry! You know that! Hey! By the way! My name is Sock to you! You can call me Sock!" Emily said, " I like Socrates ! I think it fits you better. And Mr, Socrates , I want to tell you something! I heard everything you said before I woke up! I didn't know it was you at the time . I thought it was all a dream! These last few days , I've come to realize just how much you did for me and now what do I have to do to get you outta jail?"

Sock explained the situation and told her that he would have to wait for the Circuit Judge. It might help if she could tell her story at that time, but he really needed witnesses and Butch was the only one that he had. Emily said, " Well I was there, I could testify for you! Butch told me what happened. All I'd have to do is support his story and it's the truth!" "Won't do Emily!" He said, " I won't let you do that The Judge should see through what these outlaws were up to, Running a Fake Toll Road; robbing travelers! If he doesn't, then I might have to take measures. I'll try to stay with the truth and the Law if I can. Now tell me , have you regained your full memory of everything? Amy didn't seem to think that you had."

Emily started crying! Sock said, " Hey wait a minute! Don't cry! Don't even think about it! Damn , I shouldn't have mentioned it! Let's forget it!" Sock reached through the bars and clasped her shoulder trying to console her. She took his hand in both of hers saying, " Socrates , I don't want to relive it yet! It's too soon! I want to forget it! I'm sorry!" Sock said, "Let's talk about something else! What are you gonna do here in Bisbee? Look for a job or what?" Emily looked at him and said, "What are you gonna do when you get outta jail? Amy has Butch and the two kids to take care of. She doesn't need me cluttering up the place. I'll have to find a place, but first I need a job! I've never been on my own. I was taking care of Dad until he was murdered two weeks ago!" Emily broke up crying once again ! Sock could only pat her shoulder! She had to be suffering terrible memories losing her Dad and being treated as he had found her.

"No!", he was thinking , " I'll not bring up these horrible memories again! She'll come to that on her own!" He said , " Emily, lets take it one thing at a time! First I've got to get outta jail and then we can see about finding you a job and a place to live! How's that?" Emily smiled! God that was great! He wanted to hug her! "Look!", he said, " A few more days and that Judge will get here! How about you go and help Amy bake a cake for your Jail Bird friend! The food here is terrible! Amy has my saddle bags, and I'd like you to get in them and open my folded pouch. There's money in it. Buy some food for Amy, the kids, and something special for Emily!" Emily actually laughed! " God !" , he thought , " She's beautiful !! I've got to get outta here! I can't let anything happen to her!"

Emily came to see him every day and brought more food than he knew what to do with. The food in Jail wasn't really that bad , but Sock wanted

Emily to feel she was helping him. He gave portions to Sheriff Guthrie every day. They both enjoyed the cakes! Guthrie commented that Sock was sure a lucky dog having such a beautiful girl treating him like the greatest thing in her life! He wanted to know what their plans were if he got outta Jail. Sock told him, " Sheriff there ain't no if. I have to get outta here! You don't know the horrors and tragedy Emily has suffered. I'll die before I let anything more happen to her!" Sheriff Guthrie could see the terrible resolve and determination in Sock's face . He fervently hoped that the trial would go Sock's way! Anyone that could take out Rawley Benson and Sam Barlow had to be a very dangerous gunfighter! One that, he particularly; didn't want to tangle with! Guthrie had heard the full story from Sock concerning the Indian attack and treatment of Emily. He was sympathetic , but offered no solution. He suggested that it would be good to have the whole family there for the trial.

Finally, the Judge arrived! Judge Henry Price of Santa Fe and eastern Arizona Territory! He was all business and was in a hurry to get to Tucson where he had a full book of cases to try. Sock's was the only murder trial on his schedule in Bisbee. Jake Barlow and Sheriff Guthrie stated the charge of robbery and murder. The evidence was over whelming in favor of a guilty finding. Sock's defense was Butch's statement and as his partner in crime so to speak, Butch could be found guilty as well! This was a horrible turn of events for the whole family. Jake Barlow was relishing the possible verdict when Amy started asking the Judge for a chance to speak! The Judge refused and as Amy broke down crying , little Pico and Marie came to her trying to comfort her. The Judge then asked about the children and Emily stood up saying, " Judge Price, may I speak?" The Judge nodded and she said, " Judge I speak Spanish and these two children can tell you exactly what happened when Mr. Socrates was stopped by the two outlaws!"

Jake Barlow immediately jumped to his feet yelling that his brother was no outlaw and that you couldn't take the word of babies about what happened! The Judge asked Emily if she was present during the incident? Emily said . " Yes Judge , I was there but in a coma as a result of an Indian attack! Mr Socrates was taking care of me, the two orphans and Butch Herndon with a broken leg! He quite obviously, had no desire or time to seek out two outlaws and rob or murder them! Additionally, we all arrived in Bisbee at dark and Mr. Socrates had no chance to report the killing of these two outlaws. He had a family of injured and hungry to care for! You have also noted that he collected all of their personals to turn into the Sheriff. There was loose money in that bag he could have easily put in his pocket!" The Judge was impressed with Emily's statement and unimpressed with Jake Barlow's ranting for his brother's reputation! He said, " I want to speak to the two children. Please Mrs. Herndon, will you bring them forward?" The kids were frightened ,but came forward with Amy. Surprisingly, Judge Price was very comfortable with Spanish and started talking kindly to the kids in Spanish. After a five minute exchange , the kids were anxious to answer everything the Judge asked. Sock didn't understand but very little. Emily was smiling and finally the Judge said, " The children have related to me a story of horror and miss –treatment by the Apache's and of the frightening attack by two men trying to kill Mr. Jones. This is clearly a case of self defense on the part of Socrates Jones. I find him innocent of any crime!" A scream of dissent and outrage came from Jake Barlow, but the Judge and Sheriff Guthrie threatened him with arrest. Sock was a free man! He was more than willing to accept a big hug from Emily and return one just as strong!

Jake Barlow was upset with the outcome and approached Sock and Emily as they helped Butch in their wagon. He said, " Jones, I'm gonna kill you! I know that you couldn't have killed my brother and Rawley in an open gunfight! I'll kill you and your lying lady friend! You haven't seen the last of me!" Sock lost his temper and practically ran at Jake Barlow, grabbing him by the shirt front saying, " I hope you've got a gun or knife on you! God I want to kill you so bad! Anything! Get it out ! Get it out! Fight me! Fight me now!!" Jake was frightened! He finally realized that Sock was wanting to kill him! This was a madman! He had never met anyone so willing to kill! Jake wanted to get away, but Sock said, " I'll have my guns tomorrow! You will never live to say another bad word about Emily! Get out of Bisbee, because hanging or not , I'll shoot you on sight!" Emily was appalled at Sock's reaction! She couldn't believe that someone that had been so tender with her could be so vicious dealing with others. She said , " Mr. Socrates I'm surprised at you! You would kill this man? He really didn't offend me with his comments and I think he was speaking out because you shot his brother." Sock said, "Emily, I'm sorry that you had to witness this crazy temper of mine, but people like Jake Barlow don't deserve anything but killing! I guess I'm still fighting the war and there's no gray area in war. It's kill or be killed! I'm sorry!"

Emily was quiet on the wagon ride back to Butch's place and Sock was thinking, "I guess my reaction to Barlow and his attempt to threaten me, upset Emily. Maybe I should be a little more tolerant, but that's not what I've seen for the last three years. It's been dog eat dog and kill everything in your path! I'll have to talk to her more; maybe it'll help!" Emily decided that as much as she hated to relive the terrible events that led up to her rescue, she would confess these to Socrates and maybe it would help him reduce his hatred of people that offended him! She decided that after their dinner and celebration of getting out of Jail; she would relate her story to him in private.

Amy and Butch both thought that Sock and Emily were going out to enjoy each others company and that maybe a little romance was budding. Sock was just enjoying being with Emily! Emily , however had other concerns. She wanted Sock to know her whole story and she was afraid that she might not be able to tell it all. Finally, however ; she took a deep breath and said, " Mr. Socrates, I owe you my life and you need to know the story leading up to my rescue. It's not pretty and I just hope that I can get through it all! My Father lost Mom when I was twelve and up until he was murdered last month, we were together. He took very good care of me and protected me from everything. Six months ago, we found a large gold deposit in the Cargo Muchacho Mountains west of Yuma in California. We worked that mine for two months taking out thousands of dollars in gold. Most of that value is now held in the Drover's Bank of Yuma in mine and his name. Dad was never satisfied with just mining. He was a prospector and when he heard that gold was being found in the Chiricahuas Mountains of eastern Arizona Territrory; he closed up the mine in California and we moved to the mountains just north of Bisbee and started mining. We found absolutely nothing. There wasn't even color in most of the diggings! Unfortunately, Dad had brought a bag of gold with him to use as money for buying supplies. We didn't realize it , but like honey to bees; here came the outlaws looking for the gold mine that produced these nuggets!"

At this point, Emily broke down crying and Sock couldn't understand a word she was trying to say. Finally , she regained herself and went on saying, " I'm sorry, but it was horrible! They were Mexican Renegades and outlaw killers! They captured both of us on the road to town and demanded to know where the gold mine was! We tried to tell them that it was west of Yuma. Dad pleaded with them when they threatened to abuse me. They stripped me and hung me up naked for him to witness the beating and torture. My hands and feet were tied. Dad was crying and pleading with them; telling them they could have all of our money in Yuma and that he would lead them to the gold mine!" Once again Emily was shaking and too choked up to continue! Sock was horrified hearing of this inhumanity. Finally she continued, "The outlaw killers would not believe Dad and repeatedly hit him when he struggled . They started cutting and stabbing me. I couldn't help but scream with the pain! Dad was screaming at them to stop and the leader hit him with his rifle butt! Dad moved, ducking forward; taking the hit in his forehead! It killed him!" Emily quit talking! Sock could only hug her and try to accept some of the pain she was feeling! He was thinking, " How could she possibly maintain her sanity after this kind of treatment! Surely humans didn't do this to each other! But Yes! Anderson and Quantrill did!"

Emily sat for sometime before she continued. " Yes! Dad was dead! They had killed him and now there was only me. They continued their torture and were beating me when the Indians came! I was almost unconscious. The Indians must have killed all of the Mexicans, because sometime later I was tied on a horse and carried to the roadside and dumped on the ground. Pico and Maria were dropped on the ground with me. I don't know where they came from. I was hurting terribly from my wounds and the beating. I was screaming at times and making too much noise for the Indians. A Brave came over and hit me in the head! I knew nothing more until I heard you weeping and talking on the wagon!" Emily was quiet! A terrible hurt, anger, and sadness all combined to depress

Sock! He held Emily close wishing that he could destroy those horrible memories and hoping that he was bringing her some comfort! After hearing her story and the terrible memories that she lived with; he realized that his violent anger was wasted! It would only bring them more trouble! Emily showed no anger! She had a silent bitterness and sadness that she would have to live with. He thought, " She's much stronger and braver than I am! She was a victim of terrible atrocities and here she's able to put wasted hatred out of her mind and still try to enjoy her life! I've got to learn from her!"

Sock lay awake long into the night thinking about the terrible treatment that Emily had gone through and wondered where he would go from here. He would like to stay around long enough to be sure that Emily was safely settled. She said that she had plenty of money, but where would she go? Maybe she had some other family or friends she could go to. As for himself; well California sounded promising. He'd grab his saddle bags and ride west! Emily didn't need a kill crazy Confederate Deserter hanging around her neck! She would no longer need his help!   Sock was wrong again!

Emily couldn't get her money transferred from Yuma! She had no identification and her Dad's signature was the only thing that the Bank had on file. Emily had not signed the account! She had to have an identifying document before the Bank would release her funds. Where could she get any identification! Her Dad's things! Where were they? She desperately tried to remember! Under the bunk in that miner's cabin where they were working when they'd been captured. "Oh God No! Right in the middle of Apache country!" Emily was devastated, " More misfortune! Wouldn't it ever end? Thousands of dollars in her name ,but no way to prove her name!" Sock was angry at the Bank Officials, but realized that there was nothing that they would do without some kind of identifying document. "Shooting someone wouldn't solve this problem!" were his ironic thoughts. Emily needed his help!

Sock said, " Emily draw me a map to your Dad's cabin and I'll ride up there and find your identifying documents. It shouldn't take but a couple of days!" Emily said, " Socrates, you've been wonderful to me , but I can't ask you to risk your life for me again! I'll just have to think of something else. Besides, I can't draw you a map, I'd have to show you the way to get there. It's back in a canyon quite a ways from the road." Sock said, " Emily , I can't run off with you up into that country alone! What about your reputation?" Emily laughed, " Socrates!", she said, " I love you! You're worried about my honor and reputation! The man that fed and cared for me for over a week, changing my clothes and bathing me! Look who's embarrassed! I'm going with you. So start packing!"

Sock was worried! Emily knew the way all right, but they were in some dangerous Territory. Indian sign was everywhere. He was constantly seeing evidence of bands of unshod horses travelling the roadways. These could only be Indians! Their first night out and he was afraid to sleep. His concern for Emily occupied his thinking. He couldn't let anything happen to her! "God!" ,he was thinking, "This was a dumb thing to do. Here she could get killed then where would we be! There would be no Emily!" Sock finally realized what he was thinking. He loved this girl! He sat up all night, alert to every sound; with two saddle Colts and a Henry rifle fully loaded! They were lucky! The Indians were somewhere else!

The next day toward evening, they found the cabin. It had been burned to the ground!! "Oh My God! What now!" were Emily's words! Socks were a lot more colorful! "More distress and misfortune for Emily!" thought Sock, " Would it never end?" Emily was depressed, but sifted through the cabin remains. The bunk where her Dad had slept was nothing but ashes. His knap sack had been under the bunk. It had burned leaving a pile of burnt papers and the remnants of two books. There were some buckles, a pocket knife and a scorched leather pouch. It was impossible to see the papers in the twilight. Sock carefully packed them in his saddlebag while a tearful Emily poked around what had been the kitchen stove. There was little they could do but return to Bisbee. Surely, there was some way to get identification papers for Emily!

Emily and Sock had spent the night just off the main road near a small stream. They were up early examining the papers and books in the bright sunlight. What a break! The first good news that they had seen. One of the burned books was the family bible and there in the middle protected from the flames was the recorded birth of Emily with her Mother and Father's signatures along with the attending Midwife certifying her birth. Additionally the scorched leather pouch contained the Bank deposit booklet showing ownership and signatures of both her Dad and Emily's as co-owners of the account. This was all that Emily needed. Once these were recorded with the Bank in Bisbee, all twenty eight thousand dollars of her account would be transferred and she was a wealthy young lady! Sock and Emily were hugging in a tight embrace of happiness when they were suddenly surrounded by Confederate Soldiers!

Sock was still wearing his Confederate Army hat and shirt. He was immediately confronted by a very pompous Captain Weyland who demanded his surrender of all arms and submit to arrest as a Confederate Deserter! The Captain said, " Soldier, I demand your name and the name of the Command that you deserted. We have specific orders from General Bourgland, Commander of the Texas Confederate Army, to offer clemency and restitution to any Confederate Deserters. Failure or refusal to accept reassignment and all Deserter's are to be Executed by Firing Squad! Your Name Soldier!" Sock had determined that he would die before going back to war! Socrates Johnson was dead! Deceased! He violently jerked his arms away from the Soldiers holding him and yelled, " Let me go Damn it!" He was clubbed in the back of his head by a Sergeant in back of him! Sock knew nothing more. He was unconscious!

Emily,yelled running to Sock and kneeling placed herself between him and the soldiers! Captain Weyland yelled , " Get that woman outta here! " Emily spun around ! She was holding one of Sock's Colts pointed straight at the Captain! Emily said, " Don't you dare touch him! He's not a Deserter! I'll shoot if you threaten me!" The Captain was not a brave man! He said, " He's wearing the uniform and he must be a deserter!" Emily said, "Half the men in Texas are wearing Confederate uniforms from dead Soldiers! He's not a Deserter! He's my man ! Leave us alone!" The Captain was hesitant , but the Sergeant was not! He said' " Capt'n I think she's lying. I think he's a damn deserter and outta be shot!" The Captain said, "Ma'am, if you can show me identification for him as your husband, I'll release him." Emily had already gone way overboard with her defense of Sock and she was ready to kill to protect him! She searched her mind for an answer. If he remained unconscious , she had a chance!

She asked a soldier to hand her the saddlebags from their campsite. Reaching inside she withdrew the scorched leather pouch. Handing it to the soldier she said, "Look inside Captain. You'll see my signature Emily Taylor and the signature of John Taylor. We are co-owners of this account which you will see as a deposit made a year ago in the Yuma Drover's Bank. John Taylor has never been a Confederate Soldier so he couldn't be a deserter! She hadn't lied, much! The Captain was satisfied, apologized and road away leaving a shaken Emily with an unconscious Sock! She prayed that he would awaken safely!

Sock was out for over an hour and worried Emily terribly. She was talking to him and urging him to come back to her when he regained consciousness. Awakening, Sock had a tremendous headache! Emily grabbed him and helped him sit up! Groggily, he asked her what had happened. She said, " Socrates, you got mad again and the Sergeant hit you in the head! Thank

God, it was harder than mine. I didn't want to have to treat a coma patient like you did!" She laughed and hugged him! Sock was gonna be OK. They were both gonna be OK!

Sock was two days learning all the details of Emily's deceit and she complained that he was a bad influence on her because she had actually thought about and threatened to kill someone! Butch and Amy were thrilled that they were both safe and that Emily's money was safe in her name. Butch had asked Sock what his plans were and Emily was heart broken, when he said; " I was kinda planning on leaving and going to California to look around for a place to raise cattle and horses. I've got a little money saved up to invest out there and I'll be far removed from this terrible War that I was involved in.

Butch, I'd thought maybe we could throw in together and start out when your leg is up to travel!" Butch said , " God! Amy and I would love it! We've wanted to find a cooler climate for years. These two little ones would love California! What about you, have you got family?" Sock said , " No , but there is a girl; I'm thinking about asking to Marry me!" Emily couldn't listen to any more and as she headed out the door almost in tears! Sock said, "How about it Emily, would you consider becoming Mrs. Socrates Jones!" If she'd had a gun she would have shot him! "Yes , he was

definitely a bad influence for a young girl!" A
Shot Gun Wedding is what he needed! A Blast of
Buck Shot from the Bride!

THE END

CHAPTER 4

GET DOWN OFF YOUR HORSE!

" The winner of the $100 Dollar Presbyterian Church Raffle is: Jacob Rawlings!" He couldn't believe it! He had won! More money than he'd ever seen! Sixteen years old and he was rich! His odd job work around town had earned him the two dollars that he had bought the Raffle tickets with and now he was Rich! He'd won a $100 Dollars!! He was Jacob Rawlings, the youngest son of Lisa Rawlings, widower. His Dad had been killed in the Civil War and his two older brothers now ran the farm with their families . His Mom was still the owner and things were going good for the farm , but Jake didn't feel that way.

He was tired of plowing corn and milking cows. His love was horses and he wanted to spend all of his time with them. His brothers, Sam and Joe were strictly farmers and couldn't see any good in owning or raising horses. Jake took every horse breaking job that he could get and had earned the ownership of a small Mustang gelding that he practically lived with. Moses , as he called him; looked forty years old , but in reality was under eight. The owners had given him to Jake as wages for breaking two big colts that most had refused to ride. Owning a horse and now a hundred dollars was enough to give young Jake ideas about leaving home. Those stories he had heard of the Gold Mining, Indian Wars , Gunfighters and the hero's of the Pony Express were exciting and drew him daily to dream of mighty western adventures!

"Mom," he said, "I wanna leave home and go out west!" His Mother was shocked saying, " Jake you're still a young boy! Forget it until you're older! Maybe then if you still think you need to go then OK. Now you're way too young and wouldn't last a week out there by yourself! Forget it!" Jake said , " Mom , Jessie and Frank James were riding with Quantrill before they were fifteen! I can't do nothing around here that pleases Sam or Joe. I'm not gonna work on the farm and there's no jobs around town that I want to work at. You know I love horses and I would stay around if I could work with them. There just aren't any ! I wanna go west and find a job with horses!"

Lisa could see there was no way she could persuade him to stay. She finally conceded saying, "Ok, but Quantrill was a murderer and sought out young boys to do his killing because they don't have a fear of dying. The James boys made excellent recruits for murder ! Don't be making hero's outta killers! I know that you won't be happy until you give it a try. I wish you would wait until you're older, but if you must go ; I want you to leave half of your money with me. If you spend or lose it all on the road , I can send the rest to you to get home on!" Jake was not happy with that arrangement, but finally agreed. Two days later and Jake is across the River from his home in St. Joseph Missouri and he and Moses are headed for Dodge City.

He had come up on a group of wagons headed west and asked permission to join the group or at least to follow along. The Wagon Master had told him to follow in the Drag if he wished . He wanted no dust stirred up in front! That evening , he hung out with two of the drivers, Eli and Bill Avery; at their campfire . They asked too many questions and when they got to drinking ; he moved away and slept out in the brush. The following evening , he rolled up under one of the wagons to sleep.

That bunking out in the brush was a little scary for a sixteen year old! Unfortunately , sleeping under the wagon was a bad mistake. His saddlebag was ransacked while he slept and he lost half of his money wrapped in a faded blue bandana! He complained to Mr. Ellis , the Wagon Master ; but there was no way of knowing who to blame! $25 dollars was gone and Jake had his first of many hard lessons to come! The glory and adventure that he had dreamed about was turning out to be a little less than he was expecting. He knew now that he would have to be very careful with his possessions and carry his money on himself. He would have to be a loner to protect what he had. He carried a belt knife for camp use and wished that he had brought along that old muzzle loading rifle of his Dad's.

Two weeks had gone by and Jake finally made it into Dodge City. It hadn't been easy like he thought that it would be and it looked like he was gonna have to find work to get by. He was out of food and the prices were gonna take most of the money that he had left! Down and out in Dodge was what he didn't want to be! The only jobs to be had; were Cow Punchers for the Stock Yards.

These were boys they hired to ride the stock cars and using a long pole , punch the downed cattle back up on their feet so they didn't get trampled and killed on their way to market. There were thousands of cattle coming in from Texas and they were being shipped to the Stock Yards in Chicago, as fast as they could be loaded. Many young boys and men were finding work as Cow Punchers! It was a race by the railroads to move those cattle! If worse came to worse, Jake figured that he would take one of these jobs before he gave up and went home but he'd try elsewhere first. He didn't need anymore scorn from his older brothers!

The Pitchfork Cattle Company was in Dodge. They had pushed fifteen hundred head of cattle north to the rail heads in Dodge and were ready to head home to their west Texas Ranch. Jake heard of their encampment just outside of town, and rode out to ask about a job. Ken Rollins was the Foreman and politely told Jake that they didn't hire tenderfoot kids to do a man's job! Jake was really discouraged and started to ride back to Dodge when Ken, seeing his terrible disappointment; thought he might have been too hard on the boy. He asked him to stay over for chuck. They were having a noon dinner and broiling up some good smelling beef. Jake thanked him and ground tied Moses walking over to the campfire. Ken asked him about his old Mustang and Jake said, " No Mr. Rollins, he's really only about six years old. I just rode him in from St. Jo ,Missouri"

Ken was really impressed that this young boy would take a journey like that on his own! He said, " You mean to tell me that you traveled all that way by yourself and this old Mustang made the trip?" Jake replied   "Yes sir! I came west to find a job working with horses and Moses here can do any job that your horses can! He looks old, but he's really a good work horse!" Ken was impressed with Jake's confidence, but doubtful of this old rag tag Mustang.

Ken said, "Look, do you see that bald faced horse in the cavy over there? Go over and rope him and see if your Moses can get him to the fire here!" Ken knew , of course; that ol'Bald face was an outlaw that they only used as a pack animal and was always difficult to handle. Jake practically jumped on Moses with a chance to show his skills! This was where he wanted to be ! Bald face was small compared to the two big colts he had tamed when he earned ownership of Moses. "Come on Moses!" he said. "let's show this feller a real horse!"

Racing out to the cavy, he called to the wrangler working there and let him know that he was gonna cut out Bald face! The Wrangler just laughed, looking at him and little Moses! He said not too nice, " Boy , you better get a horse! ol'Baldy will eat you alive!" Jake circled and quickly spun his loop out settling it around

Baldy's neck! Jerking slack quickly, he tightened the noose just below Baldy's jaw. Baldy took off leaving the cavy and Jake followed close behind. Everyone was now expecting an entertaining horse wreck when Baldy took up the slack. Jake closed on Baldy quickly and flipped his slack over the right hip of Baldy and spun Moses left as he dallied the lariat around his saddle horn. Baldy's feet were jerked out from under him and he went down with a crash! Ol'Baldy didn't give up easily. It took two more falls to get the message through, but in the end ; he led to the fire like an old milk cow!

Ken was impressed! This young boy was a good hand with the rope and he'd seen enough to know that old Moses was a dandy working horse! When Jake led Baldy in, he said, " Mr.Rollins, what would you like me to do with him?" All of the hands had gathered round and urged Ken to hire the lad! Ken was still thinking it over and asked Jake if he had ever broke any horses to ride. Jake said, "I broke a couple that were some bigger than ol'Baldy here!" Ken said, " You think you could ride Baldy?" Jake said , "I'd be willing to try!" What Jake didn't know till later, was that Baldy had never been ridden out and some riders had been hurt trying him. The hands were all for seeing a little fun and urged Jake to give ol'Baldy a try! Jake was a little worried! If he got hurt, he wouldn't be able to get any kind of a job, so he said to Ken, " If I ride him ,can I have a job?" Ken said , " We'll be needing a horse Wrangler to trail our cavy back to the ranch and if you can give ol'Baldy a good ride ; the job is yours!" Jake said, " Lets put my rigging on him!"

Baldy was having no part of a saddle. He was always a problem and had to have a back leg tied up to make him accept anything. Finally , Jake slapped a blindfold on him and Baldy was easier to rig up. Ken , watching the boy Jake taking control of the saddling had already determined that he would hire him . This lad knew horses and knew what he was doing. He hoped that ol' Baldy didn't hurt him too badly when he got thrown! The whole camp ground was soft and chewed up from the thousands of cattle that had been held here. Not to mention that it was better than ankle deep in dried cow dung! Jake might get a mouthful if he landed head first, but aside from embarrassment; he shouldn't get hurt too badly!

Charley Doons, one of Ken's crew; was helping to rig up Baldy and had been thrown, by this mean outlaw; a number of times. He was being a little too rough handed and Jake said, " Here let me finish! I've saddled rough ones before!" Jake started to mount up. Charley was offended saying , "Ok Baby face , you do it your way!" and slapped the horse with the halter rope. Baldy jumped sideways jerking Jakes hold and almost putting him on the ground. Then Charley jerked off the blindfold before Jake could get his right leg over and find the stirrup. Ready or not the rodeo was on! Jake was being bounced every which way and finally grabbed the saddle horn steadying himself and caught that right stirrup with his toe.

Now he was ready to give ol'Baldy a fight! Baldy was no slouch of a bucker and he really put up a fight! Jake, though; was thinking that he'd ridden a lot worse and was thinking maybe he'd taken too much out of ol' Baldy with that roping and throwing! Baldy, though; was just warming up and started bucking sideways , sun fishing ; and loosened Jake up with this surprise! Jake almost lost it when Baldy switched to high dives and spinning! Jake knew he was loosing it ! He was getting looser in that saddle with every jump! Suddenly , Baldy stopped cold : reared up and went over backwards! Jake threw himself sideways , clearing the saddle and scrambled back , getting in the saddle as Baldy came to his feet. Slapping Baldy with the halter rope, and kicking him in the ribs , Baldy took off at run away from the camp. Jake was exhausted, but proud of his ride. He was thrilled to have ridden Baldy and if Ken was satisfied, He had a job! Returning to camp , all of the hands were congratulating him. All that is except Charley, who claimed he cheated grabbing the saddle horn.

Ken was well pleased with the young Jake and shook his hand as he stepped off of ol'Baldy saying, " Good work Jake. That's the first time I've seen ol'Baldy ridden. You're hired!" God, Jake was thrilled! His first job and hired to handle horses! He couldn't get any happier! Ken told him to throw his bedroll in the chuck wagon and find a spot to light . " Tomorrow," he said , "We're going into town and get a few supplies for the trip home. You and Jim Ward , the other Wrangler out there with the cavy; will take our working horses back to the Ranch along with Beezel, the cook and the chuck wagon. Me and the crew that are staying on, will catch the Train going home. Some of the boys are staying in Dodge and I'll be a little short handed when we get home . So, Jake; if you work out , I'll put you on at regular cow hand wages." Jake thanked him and Ken said, "Have you got a side arm or rifle?" Jake said , "No, I've just my belt knife." Ken replied, "Well boy you're gonna have to have a rifle anyway. Hey Beezel, where's that pack we took off that wild cow hunter? Get that old Navy pistol and that Spencer rifle out and give'em to Jake here!' Then he said, " Jake they're not in the best of shape. We found them in the camp of a wild cow hunter that died a couple of years back out near Odessa . We buried him and brought these along with his other belongings. Never did get a name for him. Jim Ward's pretty handy with guns and maybe he can help you get them usable. They're yours till you can do better!"

Jake couldn't be happier. Here he had a job and outfit. He went out to help Ward bring in the cavy and put up a rope corral to hold the horses. They were accustomed to being held this way and Jake put Moses in with the bunch. He, being the youngest on the crew; it was also his job to help fetch wood for Beezel's campfires. Things were working out great and he wondered if he would be able to get a letter off to his Mom before he left Dodge. Jim Ward was friendly and praised him for being a great rider. He also had a few nice things to say about Moses. Later , Jake asked him about the guns and Jim examined both and said, "all that they need is a good cleaning and it looks like they'll shoot just fine. You'll need some shells for the Spencer and a powder package for the Navy Colt, but there are two cylinders for the pistol so you should be in good shape for a fight!"

"Jake ! Do you know anything about shooting?" Jake had to say, " No, Jim , my Dad was killed in the Civil War and I was too young to go hunting with him. I've done a little on my own, shooting squirrels and such but I don't know a thing about pistols." Jim went on to say, " I don't know who this wild cow hunter was , but he owned a gun fighter's Colt with the short barrel. That holster is for a cross draw belly gun. I kinda like that myself because it's outta your way for working cattle and still leaves it close to hand. We're gonna be three weeks moving these horses home so we'll have time for a little pistol work along the way. Tomorrow while we're in town , you can get an advance from Ken and pick up some ammunition."

Ken Rollins and eight of his crew boarded the train for San Antonio the next morning and Beezel , Jim and Jake were on their own with the ramuda of forty horses. Charley Doones and three other hands had elected to stay around Dodge City. Jim was running things and packed up to head south the following morning. He was gonna push for twenty five miles a day minimum and twice that when possible. He'd have to swing around a couple of Indian Reservations and hope that he didn't encounter any trouble from horse thieves. Jim hoped that he could night herd and corral allowing plenty of grazing time so the horses would hold their weight during the trip. This was the same trail that had been used twice before and Jim didn't fore see any problems. Some of the Apaches were still making trouble in the west , but the Mescalero's were staying on their Reservation. Jim, though warned that things could change overnight where Indians were concerned. Keep your guns handy!

One week out and Jake had settled into a routine. He helped Beezel with the campfire and took the rough off some of the younger horses, riding them and letting ol'Moses drift along with the ramuda. Jim liked that idea , because it would make good working stock out of some that were hard to get along with. Jake left Baldy alone. He knew that he had been kinda lucky and he didn't need to prove anything. Jim had given him some pointers in using a pistol and was surprised that Jake was a natural with that short barreled Colt. Jim showed Jake how to shoot where he pointed and explained that with that short barrel; he would have to be within thirty yards for accuracy. To always get down off your horse, stand perfectly still and shoot from the ground whenever possible. Horse back or walking was way too shaky. Jake practiced drawing and dry shooting a hundred times every day, but only fired the pistol a dozen times.

Jim told him that he had to practice until everything came natural, and his fingers were callused . Then he could try real shooting. It cost too much in ammunition to do otherwise. The most important thing was to concentrate on your target, because when you needed to protect yourself you didn't have time to think about drawing and cocking the hammer. He drilled into Jake the fact that when you drew that gun, you only drew it to shoot and if you shoot , you shoot to kill, don't piddle around with fast draw artists, if someone threatens your life, kill him! Jake had an excellent eye with the rifle and Beezel depended on him to bring in the game. He was real pleased when Jake downed a running antelope and they ate good red meat for a few days. Jim was pleased to see Jake get off his horse and pistol shoot a rattle snake. Not bad at all drawing and shooting off hand, from ten feet away!

Life was good , the ramuda was making good time and Jim Ward said. " Jake you're doing great. I can give Ken a really good report and I know he'll take you on. You're almost too handy and accurate with that Colt pistol, though; I don't think I've seen any better at your age! Don't ever use it unless it's a life threatening need. I hope that I didn't make a mistake teaching you how !" Jake said, " Jim , you don't have to worry. I never get into any trouble . I'm happy to watch someone else do the fighting and shooting!" Jim said , "Yeah Jake, I know you feel that way and I hope it never changes, but life has a way of pushing you along sometimes. My real name's not Jim Ward, but that's strictly between you and me. As a wrangler and top hand for the Pitchfork, I've enjoyed a few good years and I'd sure like it to stay that way! Forget anything I've said!" Jake was curious, but Jim's secret, what ever it was; was safe with him .

They were getting within a days drive of Odessa Texas and Jake had the first watch that evening while the ramuda grazed. Beezel and Jim made camp by a small water hole and strung up a rope corral. Jake was to bring the horses in about ten o'clock and put'em up for the night. Some of the horses started laying down around nine o'clock and Jake was thinking about herding them into camp for the evening. Earlier , he thought that he had heard horses in the direction of camp, but gave it little attention. Beezel was probably having trouble with, that ornery Claybank Mustang that was part of his wagon team. As he rounded up the ramuda and turned it towards camp he was thinking, " I should work that ol' Claybank some and maybe help Beezel out." His thoughts were suddenly disrupted by gun fire!! It came from the direction of camp!

Racing into the light of Beezel's campfire. He saw a figure laying on the ground and a group of mounted horsemen standing in the fire light! Pulling up his horse , he realized that the figure on the ground was Jim Ward! He had been shot! Another surprise was that one of the mounted horsemen was Charley Doones! Though wounded badly, Jim rolled over and yelled , "Don't Shoot! It's the boy wrangler!" Jake had stopped in the shadows and yelled , " Jim, Jim ! what's going on?" Charley said sarcastically, " We want your horses Baby Face! You give us any trouble and we'll shoot you too!" Jim said , " Jake, boy !, I'm hit bad and Beezel maybe dead. Let 'em have the horses boy. They ain't worth dying for! That's Broker Kline's gang , outlaw's from Denver and they'll kill to get their way!" Kline was a big bearded giant of a man and he spoke up saying, "Smokey, you shouldn't have talked , we'll have to shut this boy up!" Jim realized too late that he may have sealed Jake's fate. They would probably kill him to keep the law off! Jim then, with almost a dying effort said, " Jake ,Jake boy, think!!, Get down off your horse! Do like I told you!" Jake was in shock! They were gonna shoot him! They had murdered Beezel and his friend Jim! This had to be a bad dream! Surely he'd wake up any minute! He started to turn his horse. "No!" Kline yelled at him; " Boy! Damn you Boy! , Get down off your horse!"

Jake dismounted in a daze , he just couldn't believe this was happening to him! Death was coming and he refused to believe it! Charley Doones swung his rifle around pointing at him! A terrorizing unreal fear possessed Jake as he hit the ground and in desperation he drew firing, catching Charley in the chest. Swinging his gun to Kline he fired again and again at the other figures in the fire light. His pistol clicked on empty, he had fired all six rounds! His gun was empty! He was scared ! He needed that other cylinder! It was in his saddle bag! Racing to his horse he practically jumped into the saddle! His rifle was in the boot and he pulled it jacking a shell in the chamber! Spinning the horse around and looking back at the camp fire, all of the horses were gone! Riding slowly back , he saw figures sprawled on the ground! Charley was still moving and Jake dismounted and walked over to him. Charley was dying, he tried to speak, but a rattle of breath was all there was! Jake ran over to Jim and grabbed a saddle placing it under his head! Jim said; " Boy you played hell! They won't bother you no more!" Jake was still in shock from all the violent action saying, " Jim, Jim, What can I do ? Where can I take you? You need a doctor bad! I'll hook up the team ! We'll find some help!" Jim said , " No , Boy! won't do! I'm losing . Sorry I , You did good job! I wish" Those were his last words!

Beezel was groaning, he was still alive! The Kline gang had hit him over the head and left him for dead. He needed to stay down awhile because he couldn't walk straight. Jake helped him to the campfire and made him comfortable. Jake went to check on the other figures laying in the firelight! There were two, both dead! Broker Kline was one of them! Jake went out and herded up the ramuda and brought them into the rope corral. He knew that he wouldn't sleep this night and when the effects of this high tension hit him , he broke down crying.

Everything was a blur, he couldn't even remember shooting after getting off his horse! Jim had taught him well! He owed his life to this Jim Ward that Kline had called Smokey! He sat long at the campfire while Beezel slept and while he kept watch over the remains of his friend; he reloaded that old Navy Colt! Life had changed for a sixteen year old boy and the fear and nightmare of tonight would be with him for life. Long into the night he sat there talking to the dead Jim Ward! He felt no anger for Charley or Kline, just a feeling of loss, bitterness, and sadness for Jim.

Morning finally dawned to show a terrible scene ! Four dead! Beezel still had a bad headache but he told Jake how Kline's killers had shot Jim in the back. He said, " They didn't even give him any warning. Two of them rushed me and I caught a rifle barrel on my head!" Then he said, " Jim musta been one hell of a fighter! He took out three of them while he was dying! They don't make fighters like him anymore!" Jake left it there. He didn't think it necessary to straighten out Beezel! They found a small knoll where scrub oaks were growing and buried Jim. They could only leave a few stones as a marker. Jake gathered up Jim's belongings and packed them in the wagon . Maybe Ken would know who to contact about his death.

Kline , Charley and the other outlaw, they loaded in the wagon and Beezel agreed to haul them into Odessa and turn them over to the Sheriff. Jake would drift the horses south and hold up in a valley south of town. Beezel would meet him there and they could head on to Del Rio and the Pitchfork. Jake had collected all the guns . Kline's gun was one of the new Colts and Jake told Beezel that he was gonna put it in his saddle bags , just in case that Gang of his decided to return. Beezel said, " Maybe we ought to leave these killers for the coyotes and buzzards, because Boy; I hate to leave you here by yourself. Saddle up a good fast horse and in case they do show, you can get away!" Jake assured Beezel that he'd do just that! He had no desire for another gunfight!

The horse herd was accustomed to the driving routine and as long as they were given ample time for grazing, there was little difficulty. Jake was given plenty of time to think during the drive to Sweetwater Valley. He was still amazed at his own reactions during the gunfight and couldn't remember anything but sketchy recollections. He didn't recall drawing the gun, and as for shooting ; it was all a blur. Jim Ward had saved his life by hammering into him the need for practice until everything was done without thinking. Jake made Jim a silent promise that he would always be grateful and try to follow everything he had taught him.

Beezel pulled in late that evening, and it was near dark before they were able to get the rope corral put up. Supper was nothing but a coffee, jerky meal and Beezel filled Jake in on what he learned in town. He said, " The Sheriff was happy to see the end of Broker Kline. He was a declared Outlaw with a price on his head for murder in Santa Fe, New Mexico Territory. Charley Doones had evidently provided the information to Kline about the Pitchfork horse herd and thrown in with them expecting a share of sale! The other outlaw was only known as Red. He thought that Jim Ward musta been hell on wheels as a fighter! After I gave him a description of Jim ; he said that he fit the description of Smokey Wheeler , a very dangerous gunfighter from Colorado!"

To Jake , this sounded like the Jim Ward that he knew and that Kline had called him Smokey! Maybe it was better if he remained Jim Ward , a good friend that saved his life! Tomorrow, they would head south for the Ranch and try to get the horse herd home without any further trouble. The outlaw's horses were thrown in with the remuda . One was a young unbranded stallion that caused some problems until a couple of older geldings kicked him around some. Jake couldn't remember who was riding the stallion, but he thought it must have been the outlaw Red because Kline had been too big and heavy for a young horse. Jake took a special interest in the young horse and wondered if he might be able to buy it from the Ranch when they reached Del Rio . He was attached to Moses ,but this dark red Bay was a real horse in every respect and he would make a good cow worker.

Beezel was leading the herd with his wagon and Jake brought the herd along at a good pace. He had taken Kline's gun out and tried the action without shooting it. The trigger pull was very light and it balanced much better than the Navy. It was a 44 Colt and the gun belt was loaded with cartridges . The barrel was a little longer, but it seemed to Jake that it was a smoother action and easier to rapidly cock and trigger. Jake was thinking as he loaded it, "Kline won't be needing it, but I might!" He shoved it in that cross draw holster and it almost jumped into his hand when he tried it. He was itching to try shooting it , but like Jim had told him, "Practice until it's automatic and the shooting will take care of itself!"

Two more days and they had put Odessa behind them. Beezel was making good time and Jake had taken to riding that young stallion and named him Jimmy. Riding kept him occupied and outta trouble with the other horses. Moses was fattening up a little with the rest. Jake was trotting along in the drag dust, when suddenly he was jolted wide awake by the blast of a shotgun and the burning sting of a hundred pellets hitting him and Jimmy! Jimmy exploded and Jake was thrown into a small wash they had been skirting with the herd. Jake landed on his face and chest knocking the wind out of him! Near by he heard more gun shots!

The horses were running north! Someone was stealing the herd! Scrambling up the bank and out of the wash, he could see the cloud of dust following the herd! All gone ! Stolen in broad daylight and he didn't even see them coming! The only good thing was they had shot at him with bird shot and it had peppered him breaking the skin in a few places. Aside from being scared and now getting mad, he wasn't hurt! Thinking, "How about Beezel? Did they shoot him too! He was out a ways from the herd! God! I hope he's OK!" Jake started running south to where Beezel should be!

Thank God! Beezel was coming his way with the wagon ! He was OK! Jake ran to meet him and Jake yelled, " They shot gunned me and stole the horses! We've gotta go after them!!" Beezel said , " No Jake!, they'll kill both of us! We'll have to let'em go! That was the rest of Kline's Gang. I recognized that grey horse. They're killers , the whole bunch! I came back when that stallion you was riding, ran past me. I caught him up , but it looks like he's bleeding in places!" Jake was mad! Jimmy had caught some of the buckshots, but it was the loss of the horses, probably his job and the fact that this was the same killers that had killed Jim that was burning him. Jake said, "Beezel, I want a saddlebag with some grub . I'm taking this horse and following that bunch! You head on south to the ranch ! I'm gonna get our horses back!" Beezel said, "Boy, you're crazy! Don't go doing something that'll get you killed! Them horses ain't worth your life! Get some sense in your head! Let's head on to the Ranch!" Jake said,   " Beezel, I've been robbed for the last time and they've got my horse, Moses. I'm not coming back without him!" Beezel said, "You'll not be coming back! Those killers will see you and take you down with a rifle! You haven't got a chance!"

Jake was not to be stopped. Beezel finally helped him get a bedroll, food and ammunition together. Jimmy had about as many buckshot wounds as Jake had, but only skin deep and a little carbolic salve was shared between them. Beezel said, "Well, you both smell the same anyway! Terrible!" He went on with, " I wish you Good Luck! Boy, you're taking on something that'll probably get you killed. Those thieves will probably head west of Odessa and north towards Denver,but Vaya Con Dios Jake!" Beezel shook his head and slapped the reins starting his team south!

"Well," Jake was thinking, "I've committed myself now and I ain't going back without Moses anyway. Those killers will probably drop him off , the first chance they get!" The going was easy and forty horses running made a trail a blind man could follow! Jake didn't want to come up on them in daylight , but he didn't want to follow at night and lose the trail either! He stopped at every knoll and had a look before going forward. It appeared that the outlaws were running the horses full out to get as much distance as possible! Jake sighted a dome like mountain on the skyline and it seemed that this was the direction they were taking the herd. It was nearing twilight and Jake sent Jimmy into a good lope trying to get as close as possible before dark. It seemed like an hour that he rode with no sign of the herd. He could go no further in the darkness! A small grove of trees that he could make out in the starlight was where he finally stopped for the night.

Bright sunlight and a beautiful day woke Jake from a worrisome night. Following a quick jerky and coffee breakfast, he saddled up and rode to the south hoping to cut the trail of the horse herd. No such luck! Three miles and nothing! Then three miles north and nothing! There was no trail anywhere! Jake followed his own tracks back at a fast lope hoping to find that trail! He had really made a mistake thinking the thieves would continue in a straight line and now he was that much farther behind! He pushed Jimmy into a faster run as he entered a small valley hoping to come out the other end into a short cut to where he had been the night before. Rounding a sharp embankment he plunged into the middle of the outlaws and the horse herd. They had camped in this hidden valley and were road branding all of the Pitchfork horses for selling in Arizona. One man was working the ground and two were on horseback stretching a downed horse, head and heels ; while the hot iron was applied. Jake busted around that hill of dirt and the whole operation blew up!

Jake was shocked and scared but had no choice! He started shooting! The horseback pair dropped their ropes and dug for their guns! The outlaw on the ground dropped his running iron and ran toward his horse! He was unarmed! Jake fired at one outlaw as his horse threw up it's head spoiling his shot! The horse went down with the outlaw! Jake fired at the second outlaw hitting him and down he went! The grounded horse had kicked loose the ropes and came to it's feet heading back to the herd! The third outlaw had reached his horse jerking his rifle from the boot and swung it around toward Jake! Throwing a wild two shots in his direction; one caught the outlaw in the foot knocking him to the ground! Jake put the spurs to Jimmy and got outta there! His gun was empty! The horse herd was on it's feet moving away from the shooting and Jake pulled his Spencer outta the boot and fired a number of rounds into the ground stampeding that bunch of tired horses back east and south. He would have to move the herd and stay alert until he could find help .If the outlaws came after him, he would be in trouble again!

Jake, had no way of knowing how much damage he had done, but the outlaws were finished. Two were wounded and they only had two horses. One of the wounded , a gunfighter named Ed Burke; had been the leader and if he didn't get to a doctor; he was finished! Jake pushed the horses hard for a mile or more and let them settle into a dog trot for the next few hours. He kept a close eye on the horizon behind him. Coming to a small hill late in the afternoon, he stopped the herd and set up a dry camp for himself near the top. He hoped to stay awake and protect the herd. Jimmy had worked out great for the two days and seemed to be holding up better than some of the older horses. Jake staked him out and kept him saddled and close to his camp site. It was way past midnight when weariness came over him and he slept. Jimmy was whinnying and woke him! Jake jumped to his feet with gun in hand!

It was daybreak and Jimmy was just talking to the horse herd! There was no emergency! Jake was relieved. It was gonna be another beautiful day in west Texas. He hoped that it would be a peaceful day also. His guns needed his attention and he reloaded everything. Reflecting on the shooting of the previous morning , " I was just dumb lucky that I surprised that bunch and got away. Jim was sure right about bad shooting from horseback! I was lucky to hit anything! I guess I killed a horse and I might have put a bullet in that big outlaw! I hope they'll leave me alone! I don't need anymore trouble!" Grabbing a fast breakfast,

Jake started the herd south east toward Odessa once again.

Sometime past noon, he saw a group of riders coming north. There were a good dozen in the group and Jake hoped they were peaceful. One rider with a forty horse herd would be at the mercy of this large a group. Jake knew that trying to fight would be suicide. As the group closed in , Jake was much relieved to see that a Sheriff was leading . He relaxed a little , but took the keeper strap off his Colt just in case. Jim had said, " Never let yourself get caught locked in! Always release that gun , you never know when you might need it! You really only need the keeper when rough riding and there's a chance of it bouncing out of your holster!" Jake was thinking, " These last few days have pushed me into a couple of gun fights that I didn't want any part of, but right now I'm acting like a gun fighter. Jim was right again when he said , " Sometimes things kinda push you along, weather you like it or not!"

The Sheriff came up and introduced himself as Mc Donald from San Antonio. Jake told him, " I'm Jake Rawlings with the Pitchfork down in Del Rio. Had some trouble ,but got the horses back and I'm trying to catch up with our trail cook, Beezel . He's somewhere down the road ahead of me!" A fairly tall bearded and heavily armed man had dismounted and walked off to one side inspecting the horse herd. He spun around and angrily snapped , " You're a liar Boy! Get down off your horse!" Jake was shocked! What was wrong with this man? The Sheriff said , " Hold on

George! What's the problem?" George said , "
He's a damn horse thief ! That buckskin out there
was stolen from me a week ago when Carlos was
killed! Get outta my way! Boy I told you to get
down off your horse! I'm gonna beat hell outta
you and then I'm gonna hang you for the
murdering horse thief you are!"

The Sheriff asked, " What about it Boy? Were
you with the Gang that raided George's Ranch?"
Jake was scared ,but he'd had a few rough days
and he wasn't the same sixteen year old boy of
two weeks past! Controlling his temper was never
one of his best characteristics. His answer was an
angry and strong , " Hell No! I didn't steal your
horse, but I had to shoot a couple that maybe did!
I don't like being called a liar and I'm not getting
off my horse. If that horse is yours you're
welcome to him! Those outlaws were part of the
Broker Kline Gang and some of their horses are in
with the Pitchfork herd. This stallion I'm riding
was one of them!"

George was not believing a word of Jake's
saying, " I say you're a Damn liar and I'm gonna
jerk you off that horse!" He reached for the bridal
and faster than anyone in that posse had ever
witnessed, a cocked 44 Colt was stuck in
George's face! Jake said it slow so no one
misunderstood him, " You touch my horse and
you die Mister George!, If you want to hang some
one , what's left of Kline's gang is a good day's
ride due west by that Dome Mountain. Two of
them are wounded! Now get your horse outta the
herd if you want him. I'm headed south to Del Rio

unless someone else wants to object!" He looked straight at the Sheriff! Mc Donald said, " Boy, who are you? I've never heard of a Jake Rawlings!" Jake said, " I'm just a wrangler for Ken Rollins the owner of Pitchfork , but I'm getting a little tired of being pushed around!" Mc Donald said, "After today, I don't think you'll be pushed much from anyone ! Now tell me about the Kline gang." Jake laid out the whole tale from the evening of the attack to where he met them. He purposely left out his shooting of Kline, Red and Charley; preferring that credit go to Jim Ward as Beezel believed.

A somewhat subdued George , caught up his Buckskin and he and the posse took off at a fast pace headed west! Jake hoped that they got there before the outlaws were able to leave. He gathered his herd together and pushed them south! Jake didn't need any more excitement and hoped that Del Rio was just a few days down the road. The following afternoon he sees another group of horsemen coming north. " Oh No!" he was thinking, " Trouble , I hope not!" Thank God, it was Ken Rollins and some of his hands! "God !" he was thinking, " Finally, a friendly face!" Jake was one happy young man! Here he had brought the herd of horses through to Ken and he could maybe get a little rest. Ken greeted him saying, " Jake , Boy , you did it, a great job! How did you get the herd away from Kline's outlaws? Beezel had counted you as lost. Said you were crazy going after that bunch!" Jake said, " I probably was , but I just got lucky and stampeded the whole herd away from them." Ken looked hard at him saying, " Jake , was there any shooting?" Jake said, " Yeah, I was running through a small valley and broke into the middle of them branding the Pitchfork horses! They went for their guns and I emptied my Colt at them! Then I was able to stampede the horses and here they are!" Ken was not satisfied with his story, but said, "We'll talk later! Right now, let these boys bring the horses in . We'll get on back to the Ranch!"

Late that evening , they arrived at the Ranch. Ken showed Jake the bunk house and said he'd see him at breakfast. Jake finally got a good nights sleep! Morning brought a wonderful south Texas sunrise and Jake was up early. That young stallion Jimmy was making a pest of himself. He was forever fighting other horses and here at the ranch was no different. Jake went looking for a corral to put him in away from the other horses. There were a group of mares in a back lot and these were what had him excited. Ken came out and was surprised to find that Jake's riding horse was a stallion! He said, " Beezel told us that you were riding one of the outlaw's horses. I had no idea that it was a stallion and Jake he is a fine looking horse! What are your plans for him?" Jake said , " Ken , he's not my horse. I figure he belongs to the Ranch. I just rode him to keep down the herd trouble. He's a good working horse and has a lot of speed. I call him Jimmy. Named him after Jim Ward, sorta in his memory. He was a good friend!" Ken said, "Jake, after breakfast; come to my house over here. We need to talk and I need to get your name on the payroll."

At Ken's house, Jake was introduced to his wife Ann and daughter Julie. Jake was struck down! Julie was the prettiest girl he'd ever seen ! If he ever needed a reason to stay at the Pitchfork; here she was! Ken warned Jake that Julie was a firebrand when it came to temper and for fourteen years old, probably as good a horseback rider as anyone on the Ranch. Ken led Jake to a private office and said, " Have a seat ! I need to clear up a few things! I got the story from Beezel that Jim Ward killed three of the outlaws before he died. You were the only one that survived the fight and Beezel was unconscious! I want to know what really happened, because Jim Wards gun is right here and it's fully loaded! Who killed those outlaws Jake? I wanna know the truth!"

Jake shook his head saying, " Jim was a great friend. He took a strong interest in me because he didn't want to see me get hurt. I had never fired a pistol! He taught me how and it sorta came natural. I practiced every day and every night sometimes during the three weeks we were together until like he said it's automatic. You don't have to think! He taught me well! I was on night herd when the gang came to camp shooting Jim in the back, He was riddled with bullets! When they told me to get off my horse, Jim knew they were gonna kill me and said, "Do what I told you to do". I was scared and panicked when Charley pointed his rifle at me! I drew my gun and fired it first at Charley, then Kline and the others on horseback. Ken, I was outta shells and ran to my horse grabbing that Spencer and coming back , but the gang fled. If it hadn't been for Jim's teaching, I would be dead! Yes, Jim Ward killed the three outlaws!"

Ken looked long at Jake and finally shaking his head; he was visibly shaken! Jim had been a friend to him also, but Ken said , " You ran to your horse, grabbed your rifle and came back to the fight! Jake anyway you cut it , that took guts! Boy you'll sure do to ride the river with! I'll be mighty proud to put you on at regular wages! You're now Pitchfork!" Ken went on with, "Sheriff Collins of Odessa sent me this Bank Draft for $500 dollars. It's the Reward for killing the outlaws Broker Kline and Shawnee Red. They were both wanted by the Territories of New Mexico and Arizona for murder and robbery. The Reward was to go to Jim Ward or his Family. There is no family, Jim was an orphan and Ward was not his real name.

You are fully deserving of the Reward. Jake, it's yours!!" Jake didn't know what to say and tried to refuse the Draft. Jake said, " Ken, I really don't have a need for the money now that I have a job." Ken said , " Send it to your Mom. You said that she was keeping some money for you anyway. Add this to what you have. Someday you'll surely need it." Jake couldn't believe the good fortune that was coming his way and thanked Ken for taking him on. He said, " Ken, I don't know what to say. Everything has happened so fast! I promise you that I'll do my very best to make a top hand for you!"

Two months had gone by and Jake was in Hog's heaven. The one thing he loved more than life itself was working with horses. Ken had a brood mare herd of Morgan crosses that he raised and sold for top quality working horses. Ken had wanted to try breeding Jimmy to some of his selected mares and try to develop a faster lighter weight riding work horse . A pasture on the river side had been set up for this purpose . Jimmy and eight mares with their foals were pastured there. The Ranch was heavily involved in a round up for branding calves and all of the crew was out on the range when a band of Mexican Bandits hit the Ranch head quarters. Ann , Julie and Beezel were the only ones there. Luckly, Beezel got into the house throught the back door and with the guns in Ken's office they were able to keep the Bandits at bay. Ken, Jake and two cowhands were the nearest and heard the shooting. They came racing into the yard , but the Bandits had gone, crossing the river into Mexico. They had jerked the fence down and taken all of Ken's brood mares, foals and Jimmy!

Ken was scared that something may have happened to Ann or Julie and rushed into the house! Ann had been hit! A bullet had clipped her shoulder and Beezel was bleeding from a head wound where window glass had cut him. Julie was OK , but scared and in a state of shocked concern for her Mother and Beezel's wounds. She was trying to get towels and linens for bandages! Ken was going to have to get Ann into town to a doctor! Her shoulder was torn and he was afraid that it might be broken! Jake had ran through the barn and discovered the horses missing! He was sickened and in a raging anger when he found that some of the young foals had been shot! The Bandits didn't want them slowing down their getaway! Jake grabbed his guns and saddlebags from the Bunkhouse and went to the house telling Ken, " I'm going after those Murderer's. They killed most of the foals and will probably shoot the rest if they hold them up at all!"

Ken said, " Jake hold on, we're not permitted to cross the river chasing Bandits. We're supposed to notify the Mexican authorities! We'll bring the Rangers down on us if we go over there! There were six of them and they were led by that Mexican gunfighter killer, Andre Porto! Beezel recognized him! The boys are bringing the wagon around and I've got to get Ann and Beezel to a doctor!" Jake said, " Ken , I'm going after my horse and if I get stopped I'll not involve the name of the Ranch! I'll be riding Moses and he doesn't carry your brand!" Ken said, " Jake , I wish you wouldn't. There're six of them and they'll kill you just as quick as they shot those foals!" Jake said, " Ken, you've got my Mom's address if I don't get back!"

Jake was angry and just couldn't believe that there were people that would shoot a baby horse to steal the mother! These people were animals, rattlesnakes that didn't deserve to be treated as humans. The trail was easy to follow and within three miles he found the body of another young foal. This one had been shot ,but was suffering and slowly dying from a bullet in the stomach. Jake was in tears as he had to use a rock to end it's suffering. A shot would alert the Bandits of being followed! Jake was developing an ungodly hatred for these thieves! He couldn't let them get away and he couldn't afford to brace them openly. One against six were not good odds! He could only follow at a distance hoping for a chance to get the horses and try to remain out of sight. He didn't realize it, but the second day out , Andre had spotted him following their trail!

Jake was worried. He wasn't getting anywhere just trailing along behind and he had no idea what the ground looked like ahead. What were the Bandits gonna do? What was he gonna do? The Bandits answered his questions for him! Riding through a cluster of thick brush , Jake came out quickly and just as suddenly he was stopped by two Mexicans! They were both holding guns on him! One said, " Hey Andre! He is just a nino!" Andre looked at Jake and said, " El Nino, you are stupid. Why do you follow me?" Jake was scared , but had to say, " You stole my horse ! The young stallion! I came to get him!" Andre said, " Paco, did you hear? El Nino is loco! He came to get his horse!" Andre holstered his gun and said , " El Nino! I hope your life has been good ! Get down off your horse! Paco ! Kill him!"

Jake sat there stunned! Here it was again ! When his feet hit the ground he quickly drew shooting at Paco and spinning to Andre firing three shots as rapidly as he could trigger! The surprise of an El nino loco being a gunfighter caught both of them flat footed and dying with a look of disbelief on their faces! Jake was getting used to curbing his panic and doing as Jim Ward had taught him. He felt no remorse for killing these two. They had attacked the Ranch trying to kill Ann and Julie! They had injured ol'Beezel and murdered six young foals. Jake was no longer surprised at his shooting. Paco had been hit squarely in the chest and Andre caught all three in the lower chest.

Jake knew that the shooting would bring Andre's Gang there to investigate. He pulled back and rode around in a large circle till he saw the horse herd. Jimmy was tied to a small tree and the Mares were scattered around grazing. Jake had reloaded his 44Colt and had put the Navy in his belt. There was one Mexican watching the herd and the other three had gone to check on Andre and Paco! Jake didn't see any reason to be bashful, so he boldly rode towards the Bandit!

This Mexican waited until Jake was getting too close and yelled at him , " Stay Clear Gringo! Go Away!!" Jake kept walking Moses toward the Bandit! He had no fear of this man and as the Mexican threw up his rifle , Jake drew and shot him! Jake could only see those dead foals in his mind. He had no remorse for killing another rattlesnake! He rode over to Jimmy and put his saddle on the stallion. It was now time to take the mares and the few remaining foals back home. If the Andre Porto Gang wanted to give him any more trouble, he would oblige! Jake Rawlings had become a dreaded gunfighter! The Bandits were through! After seeing what had happened to their leader, they wanted no more of this El Nino!

Jake took three days getting back to the Ranch giving the mares and foals an easy travel each day. There was no sign of Bandits or Mexican authorities to interfere with his trip home. Upon his arrival, Ken was astounded to see that he was riding the stallion and had all of the mares with him. Jake was relieved to hear that Ann and Beezel were recovering well. Texas Ranger Commander Jeff Conway was at the Ranch and after introductions Ken said, " I can't believe that you recovered these horses! I know that was Andre Porto ! How did you ever get around him to get the horses?" Conway said, " Yeah, we've had nothing but trouble from that Gang for two years now. You're the first one I've heard of that won against him. How did you do it?"

Jake looked at the Commander and said, " You won't be bothered with him again ! I killed him!!" Conway grabbed his breath saying, " You can't be serious, he was greased lightning with a gun! He can't be dead!" Jake said, " When I left him , he had three of my bullets in his chest and he was dead!" Conway said, "My God , Boy, every fast gun in the country will be looking to contest you!" Jake said , "No, I follow the teaching of my friend Jim Ward, I only draw to shoot and I only shoot to kill. If any gunman wants to try me out , I'll consider that an open threat to my life and I'll kill him on sight! I don't believe in fast draw contests!"Conway was appalled! This sixteen year old boy was a deadly gunfighter that really didn't know how dangerous he was! If he lived to be twenty , he'd make a great Texas Ranger!

The summer was coming to an end and Jake was now seventeen , still a young boy in looks ; but a full grown man in deeds! Ken watched him and Julie sitting on the porch lightly arguing about the best way to train a horse. Jake was an amazing young man and since he had come into their life, things had been good for him and his family. He had hopes that maybe Jake would be part of that family someday!

THE END

CHAPTER 5

Keep An Eye Out for Indians!

She was freezing! The fire had gone out and the old Indian woman was dying! There was no one left ! Her son had been killed in that last raid at Cook's Canyon! She had been without help through this past summer and with little food, her health has waned leaving her without the strength to gather food or fire wood. It was surprising that she had lasted this long! A death song was on her blue lips as she drifted in and out of consciousness. Today she would give up her spirit! It had been a good life. Her husband had been the famous Brave "Running Fox" Dreaded

Warrior of the Apache. He had brought much Glory to Chief Mangus Colorado. Her son , had died well before his time, sadly; without glory! It is well! She was soon to be a spirit with her family! Hopefully they would recognize her and welcome her to their Hunting Grounds. If the great sun came up tomorrow, she would be gone! That final sleep was slowly crawling over her. The temperature inside her tent was below freezing. A wisp of foggy breath and a faint keening death song was all that indicated that the old Squaw was alive!

It was into this Teepee that the outlaw Ben Thompson staggered as he looked for shelter from the freezing cold. He was wounded and trying to escape from a Posse that he had outrun all the way from Santa Fe. Three grueling days and he was still running! Bad luck had dogged his path all the way from St. Louis Missouri. He had just been in the wrong place at the wrong time. His outlaw days were far behind him and he had been released from the Nashville Prison in Tennessee and spent the last six months working as a dock hand on the Mississippi River outta Memphis . He had worked hard earning enough to put together an outfit for going west and was finally on his way when bad luck hit him! No, he had not participated in the Santa Fe Bank Robbery, but he was camped on the Rio Puerco River with the Bank robbers when the Posse encountered them! He was riding a horse that he'd honestly traded for in St. Louie finding out too late; that it was stolen! Hearing the Posse challenge and recognizing that he might be, accused; he lit a shuck outta there, riding to evade the Posse.

He was pursued with Bank Robbery and murder charges against him. An innocent man he was , but try to tell a vengeful posse that! No one had seen him up close, so he knew that if he could disappear for a while and get rid of this stolen horse; he would be free. A freak storm had blanketed eastern New Mexico territory with a white out and he had eluded the Posse following a chase through Red Bluff Canyon where his horse was shot from under him . He had taken a bullet in his right leg during the chase, and although it bled heavily; he had managed to get it bandaged . Blindly following a high ridge he was trying to stay clear of the scrub brush and make the going easier. Blowing snow was covering his tracks and he had no fear of trackers following him. His biggest concern was freezing out in the open with no shelter!

The snow was deep in places and Ben was getting weaker by the minute. He knew that to stop would be deadly. Finally coming to a fairly large Ironwood tree , he found a little shelter form the wind. Sitting down on the lee side , he rested for what he thought was a few minutes. He awoke abruptly! Scared , he jumped to his feet ! He knew that going to sleep was the beginning of freezing to death. He had to find shelter , he was staggering as he moved down the ridge! Ten or fifteen feet was all he could see. The blowing snow covered everything! Suddenly he heard a faint high pitched, keening sound. At first he

thought it was the wind . It stopped! Then he
heard it once again! He held his breath, hoping to
hear that sound and follow it! It seemed to have
come from his left! Yes!! It was very faint but from
somewhere over in the brush! He stood still,
hoping to hear it again! No! Damn it! The sound
had quit! He waited and waited, his feet were
freezing ! He had to move! The sound was gone!
There was nothing but that cold freezing wind!
Slowly he moved toward where he thought he had
last heard the sound. Suddenly appearing like a
ghost out of the whiteness was a mound of white!
It was a Tepee. A snow covered Indian Tent! My
God! He couldn't believe it ! A tent out here in
nowhere!

Ben slowly moved towards the flap entrance
and called softly, "Hello, hello, Da Go Te', Hello!'
There was no response. Slowly Ben lifted the tent
flap with his rifle barrel and moved inside! "Cold !
Bitter cold and a dead Indian", were his thoughts.
Then he saw it! The faint mist rising from the still
and frozen like lips of the Indian! That very faint
keening sound! Still alive! But not by very much!
There was no wood in the tent to build a fire!
Nothing! Ben dropped his saddlebags and rifle .
He had to go back out in that bitter cold and find
fire wood or he was gonna join this Indian! Once
outside, he knew that he had to stay within sight
of the Tent or he would get lost! This didn't give
him much room to find firewood. He gathered
dead brush and sticks he could dig outta the
snow covered bushes. It wasn't much and he'd
have to keep coming back for more , but it would
warm up that tent!

He soon had a smoke filled tent, but it was getting warm inside. His wounded leg was hurtin like hell, but he could tolerate that for awhile. He needed more wood! Half a dozen trips and he thought he could rest awhile. That tent was feeling real nice, but smoky inside. The Indian slowly came alive! It was a woman! Ben was really surprised! An old Squaw living out here all alone! He was thinking, " No wonder she was dying . No food and no wood for fire!" He knew a little sign language and indicated that he had some food in his bags. She weakly turned her head and motioned to a crock bowl for cooking! Ben offered her some hard tack which she started chewing on and dug out some coffee. Water was no problem with snow all around and he soon had a bowl of coffee going.

Producing a tin , he poured her a hot cup laced with sugar! Helping her into a sitting position, Ben held her cup! The old woman lit up when she tasted that brew! She waved her hands in a "Thank You!" Ben was thinking, " I wish I had a little "Old Jack" to add for flavor. I could sure use a little myself!" He got out some deer jerky and drank his coffee from the bowl. It was dang sure hot enough! More hot coffee and more sugar later , both he and the woman were doing much better. His leg was bleeding a little and very painful. He opened his bandage and checked the deep cut that a bullet had made above his right knee! It was red , angry looking and swollen! The old Woman let out an exclamation and scooted over to look at his leg!

She was excited and concerned. Her gestures and hand talk was unknown to Ben, but he got the impression that she thought that his wound was very bad! She pointed at the bullets in his gun belt! "My God!', he thought, " Does she want me to shoot myself!" Putting out her hand , she wanted some of his bullets! He gave her three and she wanted more! He Damn sure wasn't gonna let her have his gun! Six shells she had and then he got an idea what she was gonna do! She was trying to bite the bullet ends off the shells to dump the powder on a small piece of deer hide! She was still too weak and struggling! He finished the job! "But Oh No!" He thought , " This is gonna hurt like Hell!"

He was right! She dumped the whole thing into his wound and flashed it with a burning stick! " Yes! Yes! Yes!, It hurt like hell!" He almost passed out with the pain! She had cauterized his wound and stopped the bleeding! It smelled horrible! She was smiling! "Damn it!" he thought, "She enjoyed it!! Damn ol' Blood Thirsty Squaw Woman ! This better work or I'll show her what burning gun powder will do for a bullet in the head!"He knew that he didn't mean it , but just the thought made him feel better! Squaw mixed up some kind of poultice from bark , leaves, and scalding hot coffee which she dumped in packing the wound and causing him another round of unbearable pain! He wrapped it tightly and after what seemed forever ; it quit hurting!

Ol' Squaw was sure coming along! A little food and a nice warm Teepee had her doing much better. Ben banked the fire and had heated a large number of rocks to carry heat through the night! Squaw had a number of hides that he bundled up in. "Yes", he was thinking, "This is sure better than fighting that white out! I'd probably be dead by now if it hadn't been for ol' Squaw over there. She'd a probably been dead too! I guess running into her musta been some kinda fate for both of us! Maybe tomorrow , I can get out and see what lies ahead! This ol' Teepee is sure nice and warm!"

The next morning brought a beautiful bright day with everything covered with snow! It was a wonderful picture that he and Squaw looked out upon, but it was cold! He bundled up and went out to gather more fire wood. Those hot rocks in the tent had sure kept it warm in there overnight. His leg was doing much better! Maybe he wouldn't have to shoot Squaw , after all! He needed to find some Game for food! His supply of jerky was almost gone and he had a little corn meal left, but fresh meat would sure be nice.

Ol' Squaw hadn't had a good meal in how long? He needed to get out and find something! South eastern New Mexico was not the best place to find Game of any kind! Ben was wondering how far had he come from Red Bluff Canyon! If worse came to worse he could go back and get some horse meat. That stolen horse wouldn't have spoiled in this cold weather and horse meat was good eating. His problem was, he didn't want to leave tracks to the Teepee!

Two more days and Ben was getting desperate. He was outta anything to eat and Ol'Squaw needed food! She was not looking too good! He had to do something! He didn't want to fire a gun and the rabbit snares he had set in the runs were empty. His leg was doing great! He couldn't let anything happen to Squaw! He'd go check out that horse meat! The snow had melted in places and he was able to stay to dry ground for a good distance from their Camp. This would hide his trail and he made a wide swing to the Canyon coming in from the north end. He found horse tracks coming and going along his pathway! "Yes!" , he was thinking, " That Posse had come looking for him! Looks like they had given up the search. Probably figured that he froze to death! Except for blind luck , they would be right!

The horse carcass was frozen solid. He had trouble cutting out part of a quarter, but fifty pounds should be enough to get them through this cold spell. He butchered and sheddered the quarter to make it appear that animals had been there and scuffed his footprints anywhere near the animal. Carefully, he made his way back to the Teepee. Two large broiled horse steaks later; both he and Squaw were well fed. He always thought that the meat they fed him in prison was awful kin to a Jackass! Now, he was certain of it! He hung his meat in a nearby tree to keep predators away. In this weather it would keep just fine! He would smoke some later! Wouldn't you know it; when he checked his snares , he had caught two Jack Rabbits! Squaw was happy, she loved rabbit!

Food and shelter! It was great! Sit tight and wait out this bad weather. He needed a horse to make it to San Augustine. That's where he had a little money in the Bank. If he could get that far , the rest should be easy. No one knew his big secret. Five years ago, he had been a twenty five year old general ranch hand that was laid off for the winter. His bar room friends had lured him into the easy money and He had started rustling a few cattle in the winter to get by on. Sure enough they had been caught!

The Sheriff, Jim Donaldson; came with the local Ranchers to arrest him . He ran! No food and nowhere to go! He headed south to the little town of Real De Delores. The local Ortiz Mountains with all of the gold mining activity provided a number of jobs! He started putting together a little money. Like a dummy, he had made two trips back to visit lady friends and made deposits in the Cattleman's Bank in San Augustine. He had over eighty dollars on deposit when the Sheriff heard of him being in town! Hearing from friends, that he was to be arrested; he beat it back to the Mountains!

He couldn't stay! The Sheriff knew where to find him and he was scared. He ran once again! This time the Sheriff had a Posse blocking all roads south to Mexico. He was trapped! He took an ancient old Indian trail over the Mountains to a hidden spring that he had accidentally found during one of his ride a-bouts! He would try to hide out there until the Sheriff left the country! Unfortunately, the Territorial Marshal had joined the Sheriff and he knew of this spring! Two days and they had him penned down.

He couldn't get away and he didn't want to try and shoot his way out! It was getting late and his only chance was to slip by them in the dark. He would have to walk and there was a half moon , but it would come up late! He started out in the starlight walking towards a mountain peak on the horizon. There was a bluff of solid rock next to the pathway. He was carefully and very slowly making his way past a narrow passage ,when suddenly; the trail gave way and he fell into the narrow pass way! The saddlebags he carried helped cushion his fall and he slid with loose gravel and dirt onto a narrow shelf !

Everything stopped! He was a good twenty feet down from the trail and his foot was killing him with pain! He couldn't put pressure on it! Was it broke? He didn't know! He was done! He couldn't go on! He'd stay there until daylight and wait for the Sheriff! He had no choice!

Ben watched the sun come up at daybreak and he was laying on a narrow ledge with hundreds of feet of open space below him! A few more feet and he was a goner! His ankle was terribly swollen, black and blue. Probably broken! He had removed his boot and wouldn't be able to put it back on his foot! Maybe he could crawl his way back up that narrow passage to the trail. Starting in that direction he noticed a partially buried cave like opening at the back of the ledge! Maybe a hiding place! No! He'd never make it! If his foot was broken, he'd die there! He crawled up the debris and looked into the small cave! His heart jumped! There was a pile of pack saddles and old harness laying in the cave! "My God!"

He almost yelled in his excitement! He knew what this was! The lost Spanish Mule Train ! It had to be! This was near where the Indian Massacre had taken place! Panniers loaded with gold bullion would be underneath! My God !! He was rich!! He had to think! What to do! He was rich and couldn't do a thing about it! Of all the rotten luck! All those stories of lost treasure and here he'd found it and he was going to jail! He had to hide his find! The Sheriff would get it all! No! No! He had to hide it! Scrambling up the narrow passage, Ben kicked down rocks and dirt until the small opening to the cave was fully covered! He made it almost to the top when the Sheriff arrived. Ben surrendered! Later, he learned that his ankle was broken! He was given five years for Cattle Rustling and he figured he was lucky! He really was! ,but no one else knew just how lucky!

"Yes!", Ben reflected, " Five years hoping that no one has found that little cave. If I can get there and haul that gold out , I'll be rich for life! I've been dreaming of this for five long years! I've got to get a horse and get outta here!" Then he remembered, " What about Squaw? Damn it! I can't leave her here! She'll starve to death! What can I do with her? Damn, I've got no choice! She's like family . She saved my life. She goes with me! I guess I need two horses!"

Two more weeks in the Teepee and it was time to think about leaving. Ben had been learning to talk with Squaw in half Apache/ English and sign language and learned her name. He wanted to leave her and go south to find a horse and come back for her. She was very insistant, she sign'd, " NO! Mikki toto si mew go with Hell Yeah!" Ben laughed and said , "Mikki, when you asked me if I had a name , I said Hell Yeah! I didn't mean that my name was Hell Yeah!" Mikki sign'd, " OK! Go with Hell Yeah!" " Well" , he thought , " I guess Hell Yeah Ben is walking south with Ol' Squaw Mikki! I hope we get lucky and get a couple of horses!" He was pretty low on money and needed food also. If he could get to San Augustine, maybe things would be OK.

A day and a half walking and Ben figured they'd maybe gone twenty miles. Mikki was not doing too well! There was no sign of travelers on the road, but they were making progress! Quail and other small game was abundant! He and Mikki had plenty to eat! It was the third afternoon , when a freighter came by on the way to San Augustine! Ben was hoping that they might get a ride, but this ugly lookin Teamster hated Indians and Mikki was not welcome on his wagon! Ben became angry at his refusal and pointed out to him that she was an old Squaw! She surely didn't represent a threat to him! The freighter wouldn't budge! His experience with Indians had all been bad and like most settlers in that part of the country; " The only good Indian was a dead Indian!"

Ten miles or more further ,and Ben saw a wagon parked on the road side! It was that ugly

Teamster again! This time he needed help! His wagon was broken! The tongue pin had separated and he was stuck! He needed a new wooden pin and he had no way to make one! When they got to the wagon , it was early evening. The Teamster was trying to beat a broken limb into the tongue carrier as a pin. It wouldn't work! Ben said, " Mister , you can't make a pin that way! If you like after we eat, I'll build you one!" \

The Teamster looked at Mikki and said, " Why don't you get rid of that Damn Squaw! I could sure rest easier if she weren't around! What are you some kind of an Indian lover?" Ben said , " Mister , do you want my help or not? We can move on down the road ! The Squaw is my business! She's a whole lot better company than a lotta white men!" Teamster said, " Hey, don't get so touchy! I can sure use your help! I just don't like Indians!" Mikki spun around quickly yelling, " T ISH !– T ISH !– TISH!" She grabbed Ben's gun from his holster and fired at the freighter's feet! Teamster thought he was shot! He knew he was dead! An Indian had finally killed him! Wrong! He jumped a foot in the air when he saw the Rattlesnake at his feet! It was dead! Mikki had blew it into three pieces! Mikki grinned and stuck Ben's pistol back in his holster!

Ben was shocked! Everything had happened so fast! Squaw had scared the Hell outta both of them! Ol'Squaw Mikki, could shoot! Ben checked his gun, reloading! Two shots she had fired , both hitting the snake! Thinking, "Now , what the Hell is she doing?" picking up the snake! He was a big one! She was skinning it! She was gonna cook the damn thing! "My God!', he thought, "What next! No thank you! I'll take some of that smoked horse meat!" Teamster was impressed! He was interested in a chunk of that broiled snake! He had sure changed his mind about Mikki! Ben was thinking, "With her kinda shooting , maybe, he wanted her on his side!"

Ben showed the Teamster how to bake a green ironwood limb next to the fire and cut it down to size then polishing it with a smooth stone. This made a super hard Tongue Pin that was probably better than the original! He'd have no trouble getting to San Augustine now , and Mikki was welcome to ride along! Things were working out to get into San Augustine ,but Ben was thinking, he had a problem once he got to Real De Delores! There was no way to get that gold outta the Ortiz mountains without alerting the whole Territory that he had found a fortune in gold! Everyone in the country knew of the Lost Treasure of Padro De Ortiz. The Mule Train coming out of the Mountains was said to be twelve Mules carrying hundreds of pounds of gold from the Spanish Mines around 1835. Indians had Massacred everyone near a small spring. The gold was never found! How could he get it out? He didn't know !

Arriving in San Augustine; he tried to withdraw his money from the Bank. No! They wouldn't give it to him without identification! His signature wasn't good enough and it had been over five years. The Teamster had dropped him off at the Bank and gone on. Ben was thinking, "No one to support him and Mikki sure wouldn't serve as a character witness! Go see the Sheriff!" This he really hated to do, but hopefully Donaldson was still there and would identify him! He was in luck , but Donaldson wasn't happy to see him ; especially in the company of an Indian. He was all too glad to help him get his money and get outta town. He said, " Thompson, where you gonna go? The Mining down near Delores is about done for. All the Ortiz Mines have shut down!" Ben said, " I'll try a little prospecting in some of those small streams. I might come up with something. This ol'Squaw Mikki saved my life. I've gotta help her get settled somewhere!" Sheriff said, " Stay outta trouble, I don't wanna come lookin for you again!"Ben made himself a promise that he would stay outta San Augustine!

His eighty five dollars wouldn't go far, but he had to have a horse, Mikki couldn't take walking every day. The local Livery ought to have something for sale! Yes, they had a few good ones that he could look at, but look at was all! Too much money! He needed something for twenty five dollars! The Livery Man was insulted, saying. " Mister I don't handle dog feed horses. I've got one here I'll let you have for thirty five and I've got a mule with a couple of burro's!"

Mikki was looking at the horse and the mule! She gestured to Ben and he went to her! She was pointing at the horse with cutting motion meaning "No!" then saying, "Git God Damn!" Pointing at the mule! Ben remembered that the Indians called all mules God Damn's because all the Teamster's used that term every time they mentioned mules! Ben finally bought the mule for thirty dollars and an old Calvary saddle for five. At least Mikki had something to ride now and they could make much better time getting to Real De Delores. He should have known better than to ask her why she preferred the Mule over the Horse? His answer was, " God Damn, good to eat!" He forgot! Indians loved Mule meat! "Why didn't I think of that?"

There was no need to stay in town. He bought a few groceries and headed south. He could almost taste that gold! Two days and he makes it into Delores. Folk's didn't want Mikki in their town! They had been the victims of Indians too many times. "Get her outta here or we'll shoot her!" He heard harsh words aimed at her every where! He rode on through town south toward a large Adobe building near large dirt excavations and piles of gravel. There had been a large Mining operation here at sometime in the past! The building was long abandoned and nothing but large Owls lived there. Their dropping's were every where coloring up the place. A dark dingy room was in the south east corner and looked like it was full of old freight and ore wagon parts. Digging through the rubble, he discovered in the corner of the room a sight that he would never believe.

Here among all that old mining gear was a dirt covered and filthy Brougham Landau Coach! " God! He couldn't believe it! Straight out of the streets of St. Louis or Memphis . A Royalty coach of the highest order! Here in this God Forsaken end of New Mexico Territory. He still couldn't believe it! He had to look again! Yes! It was real, but how and why it ever got here was a mystery that he would probably never know the answer to!" He went out and was surprised to find Mikki building a camp fire. She let him know that with all the big Owls , there would be no snakes or rats! It was a good place to sleep! He thought, "Damn smart old Squaw ! Now , why didn't I think of that!"

The mystery of this place fascinated Ben, but gold awaited him in the Mountains. He didn't even want to stop for sleeping. He was too excited! Mikki was in no hurry! She knew nothing of the gold and even if she had; like all Indians wouldn't see what all the fuss was about! Gold in their minds was worthless for food or weapons of war! What else was there? Ben tried to hurry her along, but only managed to get himself mad! They spent a long night and morning with the Owls!

Morning brought a bright sky and hot day ahead! Maybe he could convince Mikki that it would be cooler in the mountains! They were finally able to get underway! Sheriff Donaldson had been right! All of the Mines were closed. The Ortiz Mountains were empty holes of nothing. Mine shafts were fallen in and tunnels had collapsed where he had been working. It was hard to believe that it had only been five years! He desperately hoped that he could find that small spring and the trail up that mountain to the narrow cut out!

"God he was getting too excited! He had to calm down! "It'll be there! It'll be there!", he tried to convenience himself! He had to see it! He couldn't wait! Push on! Push on! Come on Mule! Come on! It was near dark when he came to the spring! It was just like he remembered it! Five long years he had waited! Five long years! His dreams were about to come true! The spring was where they would stop for the evening. He couldn't take a chance on falling again and breaking a leg! Tomorrow morning , he would be rich!

Daylight finally showed in the east. Ben had been awake for hours! He forced himself to slow down and drink his coffee. He emptied his saddle bags and let Mikki know that he was going up the trail, not too far! He would be back by the sun in the sky at ten o'clock! The trail was steep and he was very careful of his footing. Just as he remembered! There was the narrow pass way! It looked even smaller than he remembered! Very carefully , he made his way down to the narrow ledge . There was no sign of a cave opening! He had done a good job! Nothing but loose rocks! Laying his saddle bags aside, he began to dig out the opening at the top where he had looked in five long years before. Within minutes he was looking in once again. Scrambling and anxious he pushed back the whole top raining rocks and dirt to the canyon below! He was in the cave! There were the pack saddles, harness remnants, and old straw pads that the pack rats had chewed up for nesting! Throwing these back, he had to get to the bottom and uncover the Gold! Finally all were thrown out! NO GOLD!! There was no gold! Only an empty bare rock floor! He couldn't believe it! NO GOLD!!

Ben was shocked beyond belief! He had spent five years chasing a dream that was only a dream after all! There was no gold! Disappointment and depression; that's all he got for his efforts! Damn, it was maddening! He had counted so heavily on there being a fortune here waiting for him! He sat on the rock pile and tried to think! "If the gold wasn't here , where was it? It had to be close! The Mules had been unloaded and the gold left somewhere? But where?" He was carelessly tossing rocks into the canyon as he sat there. Then looking down at the pile of rocks he was sitting on ! He was shocked! He had uncovered the answer!

There was something under the rock pile! The old leather panniers! They had stacked them and showered dirt and rock down on them at the front of the cave! He scrambled off the pile throwing rocks like mad! One Pannier was clear and the hardened leather strap broke easily! Trying to lift the cover , the whole cover broke off! GOLD!! Ingots and nuggets! He was breathless! He couldn't breath! Never seen so much gold! He was shaking like a leaf! He couldn't believe it, "God the pieces were heavy!" He'd never dreamed what this would be like! He had to sit down! He started to fill his pockets! "No , No," he thought! " I've got the saddle bags right here. I'll fill them! No , they'll be too heavy! God, I never knew gold was this heavy!"

Finally, Ben forced himself to slow down and think! Use a little common sense! He needed money; but the minute he tried to use this gold to buy a team and wagon, everyone in the county would be trying to follow him! He needed small gold , a few little bags full; to use as money! Don't dare let anyone see those ingots and big nuggets! Take out a few hundred dollars worth and bury the rest! He was thinking later, " I may have taken a little more than a few hundred, but it's all small gold anyway!" His saddle bag was pretty heavy for a few hundred! Carefully and thoroughly he covered his cache of gold! He even covered all sign of travel on that trail to the narrow pass way!

Mikki was getting worried! "Damn Yeah" had been gone a while! The sun was straight overhead! She had taken his rifle and was coming up the trail when Ben saw her! He thought, " Ol'Mikki must be worried that I might run off and leave her! No not really! I guess she kinda likes me hanging around! I can sure get her a nice home now! She'll never have to freeze in a Teepee again!" Mikki was happy to see that he was Ok! She thought, "For a white man, he ain't too bad!"

The trip back to Real De Delores was quick and once again they spent the night in the mine building. Ben was beginning to get an idea how he might get that gold outta the country without the knowledge of anyone! He needed to find the owner of this building and especially that Landau Coach! The morning daylight let him make another trip into that back room and really examine that coach. It was intact. Everything needed soaking and tightening along with a couple buckets of grease, but he was thinking, " with a few days work and a good team of horses , Mikki and I could go down the road in style! Not to mention , that the drop down floor would allow for a false bottom and the tail Boot for carrying gold!" First though , he had to find the owner and make some kind of a deal. There was a horse lot in Delores and that was where he would begin!

The Liveryman was Rodney Calem, an old timer from Kansas and said, "That was the Torrance Mine and the original owners were from Russia. A middle aged lady, Contessa Tittle-something from somewhere in Europe, inherited the business. She came to Delores in a fancy coach years ago, about the time the Mine was going under. She left by Stagecoach two years later broke and discouraged. We heard that she died in St. Joe Missouri. The place has been ransacked over the years and the Territory will soon own another piece of worthless mining property! Mister , if you're interested ; you could probably file on it just for the fee." Ben said , "No, I'm a gold miner working a small claim up in the Ortiz! There's some old wagon parts and stuff in that building I'd like to buy for my own use!" Calem said, "Hey, Mister ! Don't bother looking! Take what you need , the Government's gonna burn everything in there to clean it up! It'll save them the trouble!"

Ben said his "Thanks" and then, " By the way , I'm looking for a couple of horses! Have you got a pair that'll make a team? I've got this one mule here, but!" Calem quickly said, " Don't want no mule! Got a good team and harness, I'll sell you , but I don't want no Damn Mule! I ain't tradin for no Mule!" Ben said , " Well, I'd kinda hoped to do a little tradin and save a little money! You know the gold mining around here is pretty bad now days!" Calem said, " See that team in the corral ? They don't look like too much , but ol' Johnson down by the river raised 'em and trained 'em. They'll pull anything you hook'em up to. Bout five or six year old's I'd say! You can have 'em for $200 hundred dollars and I'll throw in the harness!" Ben got burned on his last dealin with a horse trader and he wasn't anxious for another lesson! Mouthin them, checking feet, legs and all , they appeared to be Ok except for the age . They were a good long eight year old! He said, "Trader, they look a nine year old by the front and they're off some in condition. I've got a hundred and thirty here in hard earned gold dust I'll give you for the team and harness!" Calem loved getting gold instead of paper! He argued , shuffeled his feet, walked around the corral, complained about the high cost of feed, wouldn't be making his cost on the animals , would lose his business , his Wife would kill him, she was in love with this team! He took the deal!

Ben rode his mule back to the Mine building leading his Landau Coach Team. Turning these over to Mikki to put on picket, he rode back into town to buy feed and supplies for working that fancy coach! He couldn't wait to give Mikki a ride in her new luxury! " Imagine!" He thought, " An old Squaw riding through town in a fancy Black Brougham Landau Coach! God! He couldn't wait!!"Returning to Mikki and the Mine site, he started moving out the debris and wagon parts that were piled around the Coach. After a dirty hour of hard work, he found a welcome surprise! The coach was a road coach with wide wheels and heavy rims. It had made the trip from some where near St. Joe and didn't show the worse for ware. If he could swell the wheels , grease the hubs, and tighten up everything; he could get on the road! That gold had been safe for almost fifty years, but he was worried anyway! He found the original ornate harness in the coach floor board. It would need a lot of leather work to restore it to its original beauty! That would have to wait a good while! He'd use the farm harness he bought with the team!

There was a spring fed slew near by the mining pit and into this Ben rolled those heavy wheels. They could soak here a few days while he reworked the rest of the Coach. Three days and he had built a false floor making a huge hidden compartment in the drop down inside floor. There was a leather covered trunk in the Tail Boot and he figured to use it for carrying gold. WRONG!! It was full of fancy women's dresses! Ben knew better than to let Mikki see those! She would go crazy like most Indian women did at the sight of pretty flowing bright colored gowns! He was thinking, " Those dresses are probably rotten and wouldn't last long, but Mikki would look like this Contessa whoever riding through town! I'll keep them outta sight until we get the gold and come back!" The wheels were finally greased and mounted! It was time to go git that gold!

Daylight and Ben had Mikki up and making coffee. He was thinking, " She's coming along! You sure wouldn't know her from the frail and dying ol'Squaw that he had rescued from the Teepee! She was much stronger and looking better every day! She was happy too, and making things a whole lot easier for him on the trail! Hey!, and that shootin of hers was no fluke either! She had downed a running Antelope a good ways off! But! It was time to get goin! Daylight was wastin!" He had already made a couple of test runs with the Coach and it was performing beautiful. It was still kinda splattered up with Owl DoDo, but he'd clean it up after he had the gold inside. Mikki couldn't understand that she was to ride inside and said between Apache and sign, " Hell Yeah , you crazy! Woman job drive! Man ride inside!" Ben gave her his rifle and sign'd to her, " Ride easy ol'woman, and "Keep an Eye Out for Indians!!" She pointed the gun at him!

Ben had never had a Mom! He'd been orphaned at two years old when his parents were killed by Indians. He was thinking, " The ol'Squaw Mikki is like a Mother to me! She has no family and neither do I. I'll get this gold out and see what she wants to do after we get to a big town like Tucson or Yuma maybe! I'll have enough gold to see that she has what she wants!" The miles were rolling along. Ben had tied the mule behind and he seemed to be fighting the dust! Ben stopped and untied the mule. He immediately went to the front of the horses and stood in the lead. Ben got the message! Ol'Mule wanted to lead the Coach! He had evidently had a history in a lead team on a coach or wagon. Once a horse or particularly a mule has been trained in this manner; they never forget! Ben rigged him with a couple of lines so he could walk out ahead. He wasn't hooked for pulling , and it was as dumb as a sheepherder's setup; but ol'Mule was much happier! The Ortiz mountains were just ahead!

They couldn't get to the spring with the Coach! Ben would have to leave Mikki with the Coach at a camping spot, and go in with the mule and pack out the gold ; a couple of Panniers at a time. He didn't see any other way to do it! He'd have to use his saddle bags. Those panniers were too old and dried out! His old Calvary saddle would do just fine as a pack saddle and he could ride in on every trip! Mikki wanted to go with him ,but he finally sign convinced her that she had to stay and protect the Coach and horses. He left her the rifle! She was not too happy, but did as he asked. She would shoot anyone that tried to take his property! His worry was ; she would do it! And it wouldn't take a lot of effort or concern on her part!

The gold was still there! Just as he'd left it! He emptied a pannier into his saddlebags and it had to weigh at least a hundred pounds! "God!", he thought, "it's gonna take twenty trips to get this stuff outta here!" Then, " and I'm complaining? I'm losing my mind!" He made four trips that afternoon before it got dark. Mikki thought he was crazy! Doing all that work for worthless yellow metal! Ben tried to tell her that it was valued highly by all white men and he could trade it for big Wampum! Now Mikki understood Wampum was highly treasured by all Indians and so this worthless yellow metal must have value! She would guard it with her life for "Hell Yeah!"

Ben told Mikki the next day that this was getting to be work. He had made eight trips that morning and was grabbing a little jerky to eat on while he rode back in for another saddle bag of gold! He had just emptied his bags when Mikki grabbed her rifle! Some one was coming! Ben quickly covered his false floor! There was already a fortune in gold in that canvas lined box! He didn't need anyone to see that! He went over and unsaddled the Mule! He also checked his Colt! If this was trouble , he was gonna be ready! He signed for Mikki to get in the Coach with the rifle! It was Sheriff Donaldson and two Deputies! Ben wondered what kind of trouble brought them out here?

Donaldson rode up , Gave his Howdy's ;and said, " Thompson! Heard you was out this way. Never expected to see a fancy coach out here in the desert! That's quite a rig! Folk's back in Delores are talkin about it. Seen you drivin it around . We're lookin for Jake Levy the Outlaw! Supposed to be around in these parts hidin out! Killed a man over in Las Cruces and run in this direction! If you see him , get word to me ! He's a killer! How you doin with the gold?" Ben said, " Well , it's slow goin, but I got a little color. Look here!" Ben pulled out his small bag of show. Then he went on with, " I'm expectin to hit it big any day. This is just a small sample of what I'm gittin into!" The sheriff had heard this same story from every old prospector in New Mexico! He said his "Good Luck" and rode back towards Delores, shaking his head! " Another one of those Rainbow Chasing Gold miners, that'll die expectin to hit pay dirt any minute!"

Ben saddled up and got back to work! The Sheriff's visit had cost him a trip and he would have to stay over another day to finish hauling out the gold! Pushing to make a final trip before dark, Ben was coming back to camp at a dog trot leading the Mule when suddenly he heard an angry voice saying, " Damn You ! Get over here!" Stopping in his tracks! Ben tied the mule to a bush and went forward slowly! Peering around the brush, he could see a big bearded man dragging something from the Coach. It was Mikki! He was dragging her by her hair! Her face was bloody! Ben went berserk! Quickly drawing his pistol, he fired at the man's back! The big man spun around, dropping Mikki to the ground; and drawing his gun ! Ben triggered two more bullets into his chest! Slowly the big man went down , but still held his pistol pointed in Ben's direction! Ben fired two more rounds and the pistol dropped . Running to Mikki, Ben tenderly gathered her up in his arms, and carrying her to the Coach; he lay her on the seat. She was conscious ,but had been hit several times in the face! Her eye brow and mouth were cut and bleeding! Ben only glanced at the big man. He was fading fast saying, " Just a

Damn Indian! A damn Squaw! Why!" he died! Ben gathered water and towels to bathe Mikki's face. She was sitting up and she let him wash off the blood and dirt. Tenderly , he placed balm medication on her cuts. The wet towel was all he had to hold over her bruised face.

He was still shaking in rage, as he tried to get her story of what had happened. Maybe it would make him feel better if he put a few more bullets in that big man's worthless hide! The man had appeared between Mikki and the Coach when she was moving the horses to a night picket area. She couldn't get to her rifle! It was in the Coach! She didn't know where he had come from, but he wanted a horse! He was gonna steal a horse! She tried to stop him! He hit her , knocking her down! She got up and tried to get to the Coach! He hit her again! He grabbed her by the hair and drug her toward the camp fire! He wouldn't be hitting or dragging any one again!

Ben had to go through the big man's pockets to get his identity if there was one. Aside from tobacco and money there was nothing. Ben gave his gun belt and Colt 44 to Mikki. She strapped it around her waist! Ben was thinking, '"Knowing how she can shoot;, if she'd a had a gun on her; big man woulda been dead when I got here!" Ben unloaded his saddlebags and drug the big man's corpse out for the coyotes and buzzards! All he deserved was an unmarked grave and a cut bank ditch was handy!

The next morning Mikki was terribly bruised around her mouth and eyes! Ben angered once again, decided he would stay with her; rather than go back for more gold! Two more trips and he could finish up! Mikki would have no part of his staying in camp! She was wearing her new Colt 44 and he could get on with his man work! If "Damn Yeah" stayed in camp , she might shoot him! Ben went for the gold! The bottom Pannier had a handful of early Spanish coins in it along with small ingots. These he would quickly change for paper money and it would make it easier to buy supplies. Gold dust was hard to come by in those panniers full of nuggets and ingots! Ben made his last trip. He had thrown the empty leather panniers back into the cave with the packsaddles and showered rocks and dirt down covering the cave completely. He had no idea how much gold he had, but he knew it was a fortune! It was time to leave!

The Landau Coach was carrying more weight than when it came in. Ben could see the difference in the wheel tracks. He was a wealthy man , there was no doubt; but his thoughts were on Mikki! She had nothing and was still suffering the beating she had taken. He had to do something for her, but he had no idea what ! Here she was, an Apache Indian in a land where she and all her kind were feared and hated. If he gave her a good sum of money , the Government would take it away and stick her on one of the local Reservations. What was the best answer? He didn't know? He would get on back to Real De Delores and clean up the Coach for a trip to Las Cruces! Maybe down the road , he would think of something!

Two days later , and they're headed for Las Cruses! He had rigged harness for Mule to lead and it looked like he belonged there! Mikki's face was still discolored, but Ben had sign'd and explained to her that she had to ride in the Coach and if anyone questioned her name it was to be "Countess" Mikki ToTo Si Mew! He also gave her a flowing red dress to wear. She loved it! He was thinking , " We both need a good cleaning up, but that would have to wait until town and a Hotel! For now , we need to roll on over to Las Cruces and show off this fancy Landau and the "Countess!"He'd have to throw a little coin around to help with Mikki's royalty reputation, but she sure didn't look like an Apache Squaw in that fancy gown! Too bad she didn't have a pair of shoes to go with the outfit! He'd have to look into that! The trip was tame compared to what they'd been through and Mikki wanted to ride up front with Ben. He was Ok with that , but sign'd to her that she would have to ride inside once they got to town! If he and Mikki could keep up this ruse, he'd have no difficulty getting into Tucson. The Territorial National Bank of Tucson was his goal! Once this gold was safely there and in his name, he would relax and make permanent plans for the future! His problem would be getting through 300 miles of Apache Territory!

Las Cruces! There it was, the biggest town this far south in New Mexico Territory,. Home to some of the most desperate outlaws ran out of Texas! Ben wasn't worried, it was also home to some of the meanest and most independent residents of the Territory! The crime rate was low! The Golden

Belle was the best and only Hotel in town, but it offered clean rooms, hot baths and good food! Ben pulled his pretty Brougham Landau Road Coach up at the entrance and escorted the "Countess" to the best room in the Hotel! He sign'd to Mikki that she would have a hot bath and maid to help her. Mikki was insulted to think that she needed help. Ben finally convinced her that this would help him and she was not to talk to anyone! If she needed anything he would be next door! Ben went to see to the security of his Coach. He wanted it at all times in the view of his Hotel window and his horses and Mule would receive the very best of Livery service!

Mikki was not happy! She had never been treated so fine and it didn't fit with any experience she ever imagined! Ben sign'd and sign'd trying to get her to understand that this was the white man's way's and he wanted her to accept and enjoy the treatment! They had dinner in her room and Mikki was appalled that someone else would fix their meal! What was she eating anyway? Ben finally sign'd to her , "Relax and enjoy! This is only the beginning! I think it's called Pheasant under glass!" " Damn ", he thought, "Tastes like chicken with a lotta spices!"Mikki really liked his choice of ol'Jack for a night cap! She had probably never tasted any kind of liquor! "Damn", he was thinking, "maybe we should hang around a day or so and enjoy the hospitality!"

Three more days of soft treatment, silk underware, good food , new shoes and a lady, even; coming in to arrange and cut her hair. Mikki was appalled and ready to shoot some one! Ben laughed at her saying, " Contessa Mikki! You better get used to this , because before we're through; you're gonna see a lot of it!" Ben could find no greater pleasure than comforting and bringing surprise and happiness to Mikki! He was searching for an answer to where he should take her. He was thinking, "Maybe she could tell him what she would like to do!" Ben went looking for someone that could talk Apache. He could get by with sign talk for most common things, but when it came to her future, he wanted to know what she wanted. He thought , "Maybe the local Sheriff might know someone!"

Alan Keys, former Confederate Major; was the Sheriff. Ben took an immediate liking to Keys and explained to him what he was looking for. Keys said, " There's a woman living over in Mex Town that lived with the Apaches for years! Her name's Anna Driscoll, a striking blond woman. You maybe heard of her. She was captured as a young girl and forced to marry an Apache Brave. She was rescued when General Henry Carlton opened up on them with Howitzer Artillery at that battle in Apache Pass. Her husband was killed in that fight. She's had a rough time of it every since. White folk's won't have anything to do with her. I'm sure though ; she can help you.There ain't no street names in Mex Town so go to the Store there and ask for Anna. They'll show you where she lives!"

Keys went on with, " Saw you come in with that Fancy Coach and some Lady Countess! There used to be a Coach like that down in Real

De Delores!" Ben laughed and said, " Keys , that is the same Coach! I just fixed it up some and that Countess is an old Apache Squaw that I love like my Mother! She saved my life! I owe her more than I can ever repay! To me she is a Countess and that's how I want her treated! I had to kill a man that was miss treating her just a week ago, over near the Ortiz Mountains." The Sheriff was interested and told Ben after he described the big bearded man, that he would quit looking for the murderer . " Jake Levy was the killer outlaw you shot! Good riddance!" Ben thanked the sheriff, and went looking for Anna Driscoll.

A Mexican at a Fruit Stand pointed out the house where she lived . It was a one room adobe with a thatched straw roof and Ben was dismayed by this poor neighborhood where community out houses and a Village Well were commonly used by everyone. No one was home and Ben headed back to his Hotel. As he passed the Mexican grocery , a blond woman came out and Ben knew immediately that this was Anna Driscoll! She was a beautiful woman that would stand out wherever she was. He introduced himself saying, " Miss Anna Driscoll?" At her nod of "Yes". He went on saying, "I'm Ben Thompson! Sheriff Keys referred me to you. I have a problem that he thought you might help me with. Is there some place we can talk?" Anna looked closely at Ben saying, " I guess you're alright if Sheriff Keys sent you! No one else in town wants anything to do with me. We'll have to sit out here in the shade to talk. I can't bring a man to our place! I rent from a

Mexican woman that I share the house with. She won't have a man around at all!"

Once seated, Ben related to her a part of his and Mikki's story. Anna was surprised, saying, " Mr. Thompson, that's wonderful that you would want to take care of Mikki and she sounds like a great Apache woman. Most everyone in this country hates Indians! I should, but I was treated better by the Apaches than by the "Good White Folk's" of Las Cruces! Since, I was so called; rescued from the Apache Camp, I have been assaulted by an Army Officer and insulted by a hundred men wanting entertainment! Yes, I was treated much better by the Apaches!" Ben said, " I'm sorry Miss Anna! I didn't mean to bring up a lotta bad memories. I've had a few bad times too ,but I brought them on myself! Do you think you could help me talk to Mikki and find out what she wants to do for the future?" Anna said, " I could tell you what she will say before I talk to her, but I'll let you hear it directly from her!"

Ben convinced Anna to walk back with him to the Hotel and asked her to stay over for dinner with him and Mikki. The Coach was still attracting lookers and Ben went to insure that all of his old harness was still in place covering that false floor. No one had entered it but in checking it, Anna was surprised to find that he owned it. She had been told that a Countess had come to town in it! She really got a good laugh when Ben told her that it was Countess Mikki. She was presently in her fancy hotel room being spoiled with clothes and treatment she had never seen before! Ben was thinking, "Anna had a wonderful laugh and hoped he'd hear more of it! She was quite a beautiful woman!"

Mikki couldn't believe that Anna spoke Apache as well as she did! Ben could only grab a word here and there. They jabbered on forever. Mikki was making up for lost time! Anna was occasionally looking at Ben with an amazed expression ! Ben was thinking, "Mikki must really be loading her up! I hope she doesn't tell her about the gold!" Finally, Anna looked at Ben saying, " Mr. Ben Thompson, I am very impressed. You are an amazing man! You obviously love Mikki like your Mother!" A little embarrassed, Ben said, "Well, I feel pretty strong about her and I don't want anything but good for her! She's a very special lady to me, but she may not want to leave her Apaches and this country when I leave. I need to know what she wants to do!" Anna said, "Ben, what do you plan on doing , when you leave Las Cruces?" Ben replied, " Well, that kinda depends on Mikki. If she wants to join her people , a lot of them are in the San Carlos Reservation up north and her original home is in the Dragoon Springs area west of here. I need to know which way to go. If I can get her settled , then I'll decide what I'll do!"

Anna said, " I've asked her those questions and she says, "If you don't want her with you, please take her to the Ancient Ones Caves in the Dragoon Mountains and leave her to die in the custom of all old Apache People!" Ben was shocked! "No! No!" He almost shouted, " Hell

Yeah, I want her with me as long as she will stay! There's no question! You tell her, she's stuck with "Hell Yeah Ben" as long as she lives! Damn, I don't want her to ever think that I don't want her! You tell her , we're headin to Memphis on the other side of the Big River. Those folk's back east will Damn sure treat her better than any out here! They don't know one Indian from the next."

Mikki was quite happy with Anna's reply from Ben! She didn't hug him, that was not her custom; but she did come and place both hands on his shoulder's saying in Apache, " My Son, My Son!" There were tears in Anna's eyes. There was a lot of unspoken love between these two! She could only wish that someday someone would feel that strong about her! Ben went down to order dinner as the two ladies continued jabbering away in Apache! "Man!" He was thinking, "Mikki is really looking the part of a Countess. It'll be a real pleasure showing this grand lady off in Memphis. Those fancy ball room dresses and a hairdo sure are a long way from sage brush campfires. I can only imagine what Anna would look like in one of those!"

Later as their dinner was half over, Ben finally got a word in sideways; saying, " Anna , I don't know how to ever thank you for the help! It's been a real pleasure and I know Mikki has really enjoyed your talking to her! Just watching you two has been the happiest evening I've had in years!" Then he asked a question , he'd been considering. "Since meeting you and knowing how difficult it's been for you here in Las Cruces;

would you care to join Mikki and I going back to Memphis? We've got plenty of room in that Landau! Whatta you say?"

Anna was speechless!! Ben's offer was a God sent answer to her prayers! Getting away from that Apache capture/marriage history would give her a brand new life. She was crying with joy ! Her crying scared Ben into saying, " God!, I'm sorry Anna! I didn't mean to upset you! I'm sorry !" "No, No!" Anna said, " I mean Yes, Yes! No you didn't upset me! I'd love to get out of New Mexico Territory! The only work I've been able to get here is cleaning the better Mexican homes in town. I know I could do better in Memphis! I'd love to go with you, but I don't have a lot of money." Ben said, " You won't need any! The Countess here is loaded! Maybe you can teach her to speak a little English during our trip!"

It was a month later and they had enjoyed a great trip across northern Texas. The Brougham Landau Coach was making history and everyone in the small towns came out to see them. Anna and Ben were becoming great friends and Ben knew that he wanted more than just a friendship between them. Mikki was learning a little English and loved having Anna with them. They were camped on the shore of the Mississippi River with only a Ferry crossing ahead of them and putting that fortune in the Bank when Ben finally asked a question he had long been wondering. He said, " Anna , I've got a question about Mikki's name! What does Mikki ToTo Si Mew mean in Apache Lingo?" Anna smiled and said, " You won't believe this , but it means. "Woman with big breasts!" Ben broke up laughing and said, " What a Hoot! Mikki's chest is flatter than a snake's belly!" Ben was Damn lucky that he jumped three feet backwards! Mikki had almost grabbed his gun! Ben was thinking, "It sure was safer around here when she didn't understand so much English!" The laughter died down and Anna said, " Ben these weeks have been the happiest in my life and I've come to love you! Mikki is like family! You know everything about me and my Apache life. I know you don't show your feelings very well, and I know that it's not the proper thing to do, but tomorrow I may have to go my separate way and never see you again! Would you ever consider marrying me?" A pause, and Mikki yelled, "Hell Yeah!!" Ben said , "Damn Old Squaw, done it again ! Why didn't I think of that!"

THE END

Epilog: September 1875, A small by line in the Nashville Courier News. "Mr. and Mrs. Benjamin Thompson are owners of the famous and highly successful Magnolia Colonial Home and Tennessee Walker Horse Plantation near Nashville Tennessee. It is common knowledge that Mr. Thompson's Gold Mining in New Mexico Territory earned him and his Mother Contessa Mikki Thompson millions in this enterprise. Ben, Anna and Grandmother Mikki are anxiously awaiting the birth of their third child! Ben is hoping for a Boy! Presently, he says, " I've already got too many women telling me what to do!"

CHAPTER 6

STAMPEDE OF THE GOBBLER'S !!!

"Henry ! Henry! Henry! The house is burning down!!" The screams from his wife Helen, as he tried to come awake ! It had to be a bad dream! No ! No! No! He could smell the smoke!! Get out of here quickly! Grabbing up his pants , he pulled Helen from the bed saying, " Grab what you can ! We've gotta get out ! The whole store is in flames!" " But Henry!" she said , "We'll lose everything! Everything!! Oh my God!!" Henry grabbed her arm and pulled her to the back door saying,

" Quick! Wrap this blanket around you and get away from the back porch! I'm gonna get out what I can before the bed room burns!" Rushing back inside the smoke was getting thick and he grabbed all he could carry and tossed it out the back door! Back in again! His guns, ammo, the Store cash box and Helens little jewelry box was all he could gather! Running these out to Helen , he went back inside! Blasting heat and thick smoke met him inside the door! He was done! He had to move back away from the heat! He could hear people yelling and thought about his neighbor's next door.

Their place would burn also if they didn't wet it down! He ran around to the front of his place and got in the bucket line to pass water to Jim Burns, his neighbor; who was throwing water on the side walls of his Saddle and Harness shop. Henry

could see that his Hardware Store was totally involved in flames . There was no chance to save anything! He and Helen would have to start over ! Everything he owned , all of his animal feeds and hardware stock destroyed. There would be nothing left! " Thank God! Helen woke up", He was thinking , "My horses and wagon are in the ol'barn out back and would be safe from the fire !
"

Only one hour had gone by, but in that hour his whole business and livelihood was gone ! He stood with his arm around a tearful Helen looking at the smoldering remains of his life's work. He had been in Hangtown, California for three years and had bought out the Johnson family's Hardware Store. It had been cheap because Ol' Slim Johnson , the owner had caught gold fever and let it go down badly . He spent most of his time gold mining and his business was nothing more than an empty store front. Henry had spent every nickel he could scrape up working outside jobs returning it to a small but coming Hardware and Feed Store. Three months back he and Helen had been married looking forward to a promising future. Now thirty years old and practically broke, he didn't know what he was gonna do. Gather up what little he had salvaged and find a room for the remainder of the night. Helen said, " No Henry! We can't afford the Hotel Rooms! We'll go sleep in the wagon! It'll be a little rough, but we've got these blankets that you threw out! Tomorrow we'll have to try and put something together!"

Henry couldn't sleep! He had no place to live and little chance to find a job unless he took on gold mining for someone else! That , he didn't want to do because most mining now was underground and Henry had a claustrophobic fear of being closed in! A hard rock miner he definitely was not! He would have to search the surrounding ranches for some kind of job. Maybe he could get a freighting job with his wagon and horses. First, though he would have to find a place to stay!

The following morning , both he and Helen picked through the disaster that had been their home and business. There wasn't much that could be salvaged. A few pieces of iron tool hardware and some cast iron cook ware was all there was. Henry expected Helen to break down crying at their terrible loss, but she proved to be a strong and very practical young woman. She said, " Henry, we will have to start all over. I'll go back to the Produce Store where I was working when we got married. Mr. Williams is still looking for help and I think he'll let us stay in my old room until we can find something of our own." Henry said, " I'm sorry Helen. I wish there was something else . I hate to see you have to go back to work! Maybe we could rent the room!" "No," says Helen, " Mr. Williams won't settle for that ! He needs help and I know his business! Besides , you know ; we really need the money! There was only about $80 dollars in the money box!" Henry knew she was right, but it hurt to have to admit it. He went with her to speak to Jeff Williams the Store Owner.

Jeff was pleased to have Helen come back to work, although he expressed great concern for the loss of their business. He had promised the room to a border that was moving to Hangtown from Sacramento to go to work in his store. Helen and Henry could use it until the worker arrived. They would have to move out in forty five days. Henry was grateful for the time. It would give them a chance to try and get something together. He told Helen to take the money and get what they would need for food and clothing. He would get a horse and ride out to some of his Ranching customers and see about work or a job.

Work was scarce, but Henry found a hauling job that looked promising. John Rutgars was a poultry grower that normally bought all of his feed from Henry and he was in need of a wagon load. Henry , then contracted with Rutgars to deliver a load from the nearest mill on the   River about fifty miles away. The only problem was, Rutgars would have to pay in trade. Henry would get poultry instead of money. Henry hurried back to town and readied his wagon and team. Helen was not too pleased with chickens instead of dollars, but Henry convinced her that it was better than nothing. He was to get $20 dollars for the delivery and that amounted to 60 chicken culls from Rutgars flock. Henry then asked Helen about selling them to store customers. Helen thought that was a great idea. She would take orders and sell then in town.

Four days later, Henry and Helen were in the Poultry for Sale business. Henry had built a holding pen in his little barn and was keeping them well fed and sheltered until a customer ordered one. Chickens became a profitable income for Henry, because almost every Rancher had a flock and was willing to trade poultry , especially roosters, for hauling fees. While Henry was hauling, Helen had been busy setting up a place in the barn where she could kill and clean chickens! She was earning twenty five cents apiece above the $1 dollar per head that they sold for alive! Their savings was growing and they had talked about eventually rebuilding their store. First, though; they had to find a place to live. It was mid summer and they still had about twenty days before they had to move.

Henry had picked up a long haul job to Carson City, Nevada and it promised to pay a good months wages. He would get $50 dollars for the trip to pick up a small three stamp mill from a gold mine outside of Carson. This meant that he would be taking an empty wagon over the pass going east. He and Helen had forty some chickens in the barn and Henry decided to crate them on his wagon and take them to Carson City along with five old tom turkey's that he had acquired in trade. Jackson Cut Off was the route he had chosen because it was about forty miles shorter.

When he stopped at the Johnson House near the crest of the Sierra Carson Pass, Mister Johnson's wife bought two of his turkeys for four dollars each. Henry had priced them at this figure , thinking that he would be lucky to get two dollars for old Toms. He was really surprised that

Molly Johnson grabbed them at his price! She also paid two dollars apiece for half a dozen chickens! He was thinking that maybe he'd have to raise his prices a little, if poultry was that much in demand!

Arriving in Carson City, he found that almost everyone ate pork, beans , hot bread and coffee three times a day. These folks were anxious for chicken and turkey at any reasonable price. All of his chickens and turkey's were sold before he hit the livery stable. Locating the Broken Spade Gold Mine and loading the stamp mill was a short job and Henry was ready to head home. He had sold his turkey's for five dollars each and everyone wanted to know if he was going to be bringing more. People in Carson City were starving for poultry and beef. Henry was trying to figure out how he could take advantage of this market demand where he could far more than double his money practically overnight! He needed to bring a herd of cattle into Carson and he could become wealthy overnight. The Comstock Mines were booming and prices were sky high everywhere. His problem , of course was; he needed money to buy livestock and he had very little. Buying beef cattle for resale butcher was completely out of his realm of finance! " Still!," he was thinking, "the prospects are too attractive. He had to think of something!"

Halfway up to the Carson Summit, he over took a Mexican with a pack burro and two small dogs climbing the grade. When he got closer , he realized that the burro was also carrying two small boys. His team needed a breather so he pulled over and spoke to the Mexican, asking him , " Hey!, would you like a lift to the top of the grade? I'm gonna give my team a short breather, but my load is not too bad and if you'd like a lift , get on board." The Mexican spoke good English and they exchanged names. He was Rudolpho (Rudy) Oterro and he was heading into Placerville and on into Sacramento.

Henry was glad for the company and when they reached the top of the grade , he asked the boy's to climb aboard also. The burro was tied to the tailgate and walked along behind. The two small dogs trotted along near the wagon. The boys were seven year old Ricky and five year old Robbie. Henry was enjoying their chatter, half Spanish and half English. He learned that their Mom had died the past winter and they went with Rudy everywhere. He had no place to leave them and was trying to get to Sacramento where his brother's family lived. There, maybe he could leave the boys while he found work. Things were pretty rough for him at the moment.

Henry was curious about the two dogs. If Rudy couldn't take care of his boys, why the dogs? Rudy said, " They're herding dogs and with the number of sheep in the Valley area. I can very easily get a job. These dogs will make me a good living. That's another reason I'm headed for Sacramento!" Henry asked, "Are you planning on leaving the boys while you take a herding job? Seems like you won't be seeing much of them for the rest of the summer!" Rudy answered, "Yes, but I have no choice. I can't keep them with me herding sheep. I just hope that my brother's wife is OK with leaving them there. If not, I don't know what I'll do!" Henry said, " look, Rudy, you can bunk in my barn for a couple of days in Hangtown and look around a little. Maybe something will come up. In the meantime , I could use a little help delivering this Stamp Mill." Rudy was thankful for the offer and more than willing to help with the delivery and unloading.

Henry was worried about Helen's response at having two little boys around , but she was thrilled to fix for them and seemed to be delighted that he tried to help the family! She was not too happy that they would have to live in the barn, but Henry assured her that it was far better than what they had been accustomed to. He kinda got the feeling that she would be OK with him sleeping in the barn and the kids staying with her. Now this was going a bit too far! The kids stayed with their Dad. Henry had Rudy leave the dogs and burro at the barn , while they and the kids delivered the Stamp Mill.

Charley Jackson was the owner of the Buck Horn Mining Company that had purchased and paid for delivery of the Stamp Mill. The quartz seam he was working seemed to be quite productive and he was anxious to crush some ore and process some gold. Rudy hit him up for a job, but Charley wasn't hiring until the assessments came in; and only then if the findings were high grade! Henry noted that the Mining company property was over run with turkeys and asked

Charley, "Are these all wild turkeys running around here or are you raising them?" Charley answered , "No they belong to my Father in Law, Jim Lawler. He was in the business last year, but has since given it up. He couldn't sell the damn things and this year they've taken over the place. Most of them are practically wild. There must be hundreds of them living in the woods around here!"

Henry was looking at dollars on the hoof or turkey foot! He said to Charley, " Do you reckon your Father in Law Jim, would take fifty cents apiece for what I could catch? I could take the fifty dollar hauling fee and trade it for turkeys and I'll do the catching!" Charley said, " He might not , but I damned sure will! I'd love to get rid of the messy and noisy things ! Henry , you bring your traps and you've got a deal!" Henry told him, " It'll take me a couple of days to get cages together but we'll be back by the end of this week!"

Later Henry said to Rudy, " Well do you want a job catching and hauling turkeys? I can probably pay $5 dollars a week for the help!" Rudy was OK with that arrangement, especially since he had a place to stay with the pay. Henry hurried back to Hangtown and told Helen of the agreement. She was a little apprehensive of risking the fifty dollars buying turkeys, but Henry was excited with the prospects. He started forming plans to build cages and trap turkeys!

Four days later with a wagon load of cages, he and Rudy drove to Charley's Buck Horn Mining Office and set out to capture a group of turkeys.

Henry knew a little bit about turkeys and arrived in the late afternoon. He had brought a sack of corn with him to entice the birds and they came running to the shelters and sheds that they had been raised in. Scattering a little corn about , the birds feverishly grabbed the kernels and went to roost. Henry and Rudy went about collecting a hundred Jakes (this year's Tom's) and mixed hens . Henry said to Rudy, "Don't get any of those big Tom's. They'll take up too much room in the cages." When they left , Charley was very pleased with the trade. Henry told him that if this trip went off well, he'd be back for more turkeys. Charley wished him "Good Luck".

Henry had made a big mistake! He realized this as they pulled out of the Mining Yard. That poor wagon of his was overloaded and his team was having trouble pulling through the deep sand. One hundred turkeys at ten to fifteen pounds each had pushed his wagon and load to way over a ton for his two horses. They were struggling and Henry knew that he would never be able to take a load such as this over the pass to Carson City! He would have to figure out a different plan or eat turkey for the next two years! Two hours later ,following many rest stops with he and Rudy walking ; they finally made it into their barn area. Henry felt that he needed to somehow find buyers for his flock of turkeys before they ate him out of all of his projected profits!

The following morning, Henry released some of his birds and watched them scattering out over the surrounding fields eating grasshoppers. Hey!

This was Ok! Maybe his feed bill wouldn't be that bad after all! There were thousands of grasshoppers around! He kept about twenty of the hens penned up so the free birds would keep a home base. He said to Rudy, " I don't know just yet how we'll get these birds to Carson, but we have to figure out something. I can sell a few ,here in Hangtown ,but Carson is where the money is!"

That evening, Henry was worried. About twenty five of his Jakes were staying a good hundred yards out from his barn and it looked like they might be looking to roost in the local trees. Rudy said, " Henry, maybe I could send the dogs down to bring them in." Henry said, " Go ahead, it might work!" Sure enough, those two little dogs worked those turkeys right into the barn! Henry had never seen anything like it. Rudy had whistled and hand signaled those dogs just like herding sheep and all hundred were now roosting in the barn! Henry now knew how he would get those birds to Carson! If those dogs could herd these turkeys, he would walk some to the top of the Pass and let them ride to the bottom.

The following week Henry and Rudy took the two dogs, the burro and one hundred turkeys to Carson. Helen agreed to take care of the two boys. Pedro, the burro carried two sacks of corn. They had a good one hundred and twenty miles to travel and it looked like a good week to ten days getting there. The first day out , they camped early and let the birds out to feed and water near a small creek. The birds all roosted in or on the wagon leaving it a splattered mess. Henry, Rudy and the animals roosted (camped) a little upstream! This was to be their daily routine until they hit the pass. When the High Sierra climb started , Henry let most of the birds out and the dogs kept them closely following the wagons. Traffic on this cutoff Pass was very heavy and frequently, they had to move off the roadway to permit drovers and wagons to pass. Herding was very difficult and made for a lot of wasted time gathering the birds after they were scattered by some folks even shooting at them! Fortunately, they suffered no losses and finally made it to the top of the Pass. Going downhill posed another problem. The wooden wheel brakes were smoking and Henry hooked a downed tree to the wagon and dragged it behind to provide some breaking action. The dust was pretty bad ,but didn't seem to bother the birds.

On the flats at last and headed up the valley to Carson, his turkeys were selling to everyone for five dollars each. He never made it to Carson City. He was outta turkeys at ten miles out! He had turned fifty dollars into almost five hundred. It was time to return home and get another load of turkeys! Henry knew though that he would have to devise a new scheme to get turkeys to Carson. His wagon needed extensive repairs and wouldn't handle that kind of abuse again! A new wagon was outta the question . There had to be a better way.

Helen was overjoyed at the success of this venture and wanted Henry to rent a house and immediately begin rebuilding his Store. Henry had other ideas and wanted to make another trip to Carson. He said to Helen, " Hon , I don't think that I want to rebuild. I spent the last three years running this small business and never had the opportunity to earn the kind of money we made this last week. I worked all year and didn't make one hundred dollars that I could put in the bank. I'd like to buy another large flock of turkeys and try herding them to Carson. Rudy and you could help and we would just camp out as we went down the road."

Helen said , "Henry, you're crazy! Whoever heard of doing such a thing? You'd have birds scattered for a hundred miles and every Bobcat and coyote in the country would be feeding off your flock!" Henry said, " No Helen, you're wrong! Rudy and I trailed that one hundred birds all the way up and over the Sierra Summit and never lost a bird. I know that we walked that bunch at least seventy five miles. If I can sell the lot and barn here in town , I'll take most of the money and buy every turkey I can get and head for Carson. We won't come back to Hangtown!"

"Rudy has a place in the San Simon Valley in southern Arizona that is part of an old Spanish Ranch that we can buy a half interest in. If we can get enough turkeys and if we can get them to Carson, we'll have enough money to really build you a beautiful home and buy the ranch." Helen was appalled that Henry was even thinking such a thing! " What about these two little boys? Where will they go? Who will take care of them? You're risking everything that we have! I still think you're out of your mind!" Henry tried to explain, "Helen," he said, " We lost everything in the fire except our wagon and eighty dollars! I know it's risky, but we have an opportunity here to set ourselves and Rudy and the boys up for life! Rudy is ready and anxious to give it a try! It'll be hard work for you, I know; but I think we can do it. The boys will ride Pedro and stay in front of the flock . They can scatter a little corn when we need to move the birds quickly. You can drive the wagon with a full load of corn and the supplies that we'll need on the trail. Rudy and I will walk behind with the dogs. Do you think you can do that?"

Helen was hesitant to even give Henry an answer, but finally thinking it over she said, " OK, in some ways you're right. We don't have much of anything and I guess we couldn't be much worse off. Yes ,I can drive the wagon, but we'll need a lot more than what you and Rudy took on your last trip! If we're gonna go all the way to southern Arizona, then we need to plan for that trip also." Henry knew then that he'd surely married the right kind of a woman. It would be much harder on her than on him and Rudy, but if things worked out as he planned ; he'd sure make it up to her. He was thinking that maybe the thought of a beautiful home was enough to persuade her. He also knew that since she decided to go along, you had best get out of her way. It was time to get that wagon back in good condition and stock it with Helen stuff!

Money was hard to come by and Henry found that no one wanted to buy his burned out lot and barn. He even offered it to his neighbor for a low three hundred dollars, but nix; there was no interest. He needed to ride out to see Charley and check on buying up more turkeys. He would need to form some kind of plan to move a few hundred birds. Their money was down to about four hundred and Henry had purchased everything for the trip.

Charley said that he had about fifteen to eighteen hundred turkeys. Jim Lawler, his father in law; insisted there was over two thousand and he wanted to sell them all! Henry told them both that he didn't have that kind of money, but he was willing to throw his lot and barn in town into the deal for a turkey trade. Charley was all for a straight out swap for four hundred plus the town property. Henry was afraid that Jim and Charley were gonna fight each other over the deal until Charley reminded Jim that they had a two hundred dollar feed bill over due and it would get worse. If they quit throwing out the feed this bunch of turkeys would disappear into the surrounding country side and they wouldn't have any to sell!

The deal was settled. Henry now owned a bunch of turkeys! How many? He had no idea! It was time to pack his family on the wagon and start moving turkeys! Hopefully there would be enough to make him the money needed for the ranch. Helen was ready to leave. She had been living out of the wagon and barn for two days because her replacement had come in from Sacramento. Her job now was taking care of two little boys and cooking meals for Henry and Rudy. She and Henry were quite excited about the coming trip and risky adventure they were about to jump into! Everything was in readiness except the turkeys.

At daybreak , Henry, Rudy, Helen and company had arrived to start the turkeys down the road. The turkeys were not yet ready to leave! Jim told them, " You can't tell about these birds. They'll come down off their roosts when they're ready and not before. Just sit tight for a bit and when one comes down they'll all come down!" Half an hour later the birds were still content to sit right where they were. Henry was getting more than a little upset. He wanted to get down the road! This delay was gonna cost him a day if they didn't get going!

One old hen flew down!! None of them had ever witnessed the action that took place next! It appeared that thousands of noisy birds descended from the roosts and local trees all at once! There were hundreds everywhere, all headed for the empty feeders. This was the plan that Henry had set up with Jim. Robbie and Ricky rode forward on Pedro throwing out small hands full of corn. The birds eagerly followed scooping up everything that hit the ground and running to stay close to Pedro. The surrounding yard was a sea of turkeys, all trying to get close to a couple of scared little boys riding a burro! Helen drove her wagon forward and the trek to Carson City was underway. Henry and Rudy followed behind with the two little dogs.

Once clear of the Mining Compound, the boys cut back on the corn and the birds followed along hoping for a kernel now and then. Henry had no idea how many birds they had. It surely looked like the two thousand or so that Jim had estimated. Things went well as they went down the road. The birds were running out catching grasshoppers and anything else they came across. Henry was well pleased with the fact that the birds had settled down and followed ol'Pedro like he was the Pied Piper. He was the source of food and they hung close. A few ranch dogs came out to run at the birds barking and some took to the air for short distances, but shortly landed and merged back into the herd.

They had traveled maybe ten miles when they came to a large open pasture and Henry decided to stop and give the birds a rest from the hike! The birds scattered like quail over the pasture and Henry thought that he had made a grave error! Luckily he was wrong! The birds were gobbling up grasshoppers! They loved those things! Within an hour, the birds were fully fed and ready to head down the road. Night time and at dusk they were a good twenty five miles closer to Carson city. Coming into a small grove of trees near a river, the birds all decided to go to roost. In ten minutes there wasn't a bird left on the ground!

Everyone was ready for a good nights rest. Henry and Rudy built a campfire and the boys helped Helen cook their supper. Things were starting to come together like Henry hoped that they would. He wasn't ready to start counting his money yet, but things were sure looking good to this point! Rudy had tried to get a count of the turkeys, but admitted that the closest he could come was somewhere between a large and a big bunch! They moved around so much that there was no way to get even an estimate. Looking at all of the low branches of the trees, they were loaded and all of the birds were out of the reach of predators.

A beautiful sunrise met them after daybreak and it was time to grab breakfast and start herding turkeys! The river was about twenty yards across and pretty shallow at the crossing. Turkeys do not like water and if you had any ideas about them wading or swimming, you were dreaming! Henry and Rudy had a little experience with this problem because they had faced it in their earlier trip to Carson. Helen was quite interested in how they were gonna get these birds to cross that river! Henry was gonna demonstrate. Loading one of their cages with corn , it was easy to trap a dozen birds inside. Then he asked Helen to drive the team across and release the birds on the far shore. It was his plan that the others would then fly across to "join their brethren on the yonder shore"! Well, to a degree, the plan worked great, except for one slight problem! The birds released on the far yonder shore flew back to join their brethren on the shore they had just left!!

It was frustrating and called for Plan B, if there was one. Henry called Helen back and then sent Ricky and Robbie over with Pedro and the loose corn. A little yelling by the boys and after throwing out a little grain, them hundreds of birds flew over and decended on the two boys. Once again they were scared to death. Even ol'Pedro took off in a slow run to escape the turkey deluge! Henry had forgot what Jim had told him about turkey eyesight. These birds could see a grasshopper at fifty yards and go catch it! He had no need of luring them with anything other than corn! The rest of the day saw no further incidents. They were coming up into the foot hills and after crossing two more small streams , Henry decided to strike camp early and let the birds forage for food before nightfall. There was a grove of trees handy and it was a perfect camping ground.

Morning once again and this time Henry hoped for an earlier start. Sending the boys out right after breakfast brought them turkeys down chasing after ol'Pedro. A few light sprinklings of corn and the whole camp was on the move! Approaching the Sierra Pass, Henry conferred with Rudy and decided to take the old Emigrant Trail going over the Pass , rather than the Johnson House Cutoff. It would be twenty miles further and cost another good day, but there would be no traffic to contend with.

Grasshoppers were thick and those turkeys were feasting ! There appeared to be some kind of Dragonfly hatch and birds were chasing these everywhere. There was a constant fight between turkeys to grab the insects! It was getting colder the further up the mountain that they went and the insects thinned out. The next day, Henry figured to throw out a little more corn. Those birds were gonna be real hungry by the time they passed the snow line on top! He stopped once again in a thick grove of trees to spend a cold night .Those birds huddled close together and he and Rudy built up a large camp fire to spread a little heat for themselves.

The following morning everyone , including the turkeys were anxious to get down off that mountain. Around ten o'clock, they had dropped down to a sharp cliff and slide formation that ran parallel to the trail. There was nothing for hundreds of feet down and the turkeys stopped at this upper cliff edge. Henry sent the boys on down with corn encouragement, but this time those silly birds weren't buying the lure. They were afraid of that cliff and wouldn't string out to go down that narrow trail that the boys and ol'Pedro were traveling.

Helen was in back with the wagon and Rudy sent the little dogs in to push the birds along. Henry moved in and brought Helen in closer and they all pressured those birds to move out. Suddenly they did!! The whole flock took off flying and all hundreds of them flew down that mountain and out of sight! Henry was devastated! He had lost everything! He and Helen sat there in shock as they watched their dreams fly off to God knows where!! Everything, they had was tied up in those birds and now they were gone, every single last one of them! Helen could only set there and cry. They had lost it all! Not one stinking Gobbler left!

Henry was destroyed! What Now! He forlornly , walked down that mountainside with a saddened

Rudy. All their plans ruined by those turkeys going wild on them after getting this far! They were over half way to Carson! There was not a turkey in sight! Gone! He couldn't get over it! All that work and all for nothing! Then he heard it! A turkey gobbled in the distance! More gobbling and then rounding a corner in the trail! There they were, all scattered out over the valley floor chasing grasshoppers! " My God ! My God!" was all he could say! It was time to stop and be thankful for finding all of their turkeys safe in the valley. Helen, following close behind was crying again, but this time tears of joy, Ricky and Robbie were clapping and even ol'Pedro seemed happy to see all the birds! It was a joyful and happy camp that evening. Then the Indians came!!

Six families of Indians , Braves, Squaws, a passel of kids and they were all looking hungrily at that forest full of turkeys!! Henry and Helen had the same thoughts, " We'll have to feed this bunch or they'll take what they want!" Henry invited them all to the campsite and sent Rudy out with Robbie to shoot three of the big Toms out of the trees. Less than half an hour later , turkey was roasting over the big camp fire. All had a good feast and the Indians were grateful for the meal. Henry and Rudy were some concerned ,but the evening and night went without incident.

Another beautiful sunrise and all the birds are on the ground chasing grasshoppers. Rudy was good with sign language and said to Henry, "The Indians want some birds to take with them. They're willing to trade. They have a spare horse.

Would you be willing to trade?" Henry checked out the horse. It was a small Mustang and appeared to be young and healthy. Thinking that if they went on to southern Arizona, Rudy could use a horse. He traded for four turkeys! The Indians tied their birds to their horses and left. Henry hurried things along, his turkeys had been held ,up long enough and he didn't want to keep those hungry folk's in Carson waiting! The little Mustang was a good ride and he traded off with Rudy getting a little rest for his weary feet.

Heading up Carson River , he noted that this time of year it should have been called a creek. The country was flat and trees were getting scarce. As dark approached , the turkeys were looking for a place to roost! Henry was getting worried that they would all try the wagon and smother each other piling up. He could see a few sheds and buildings just west of the road and remembered from his previous trips that it was an old Pony Express Station.

He sent Rudy and the boys with Pedro in that direction herding his multitude of gobblers behind! As they approached hundreds of birds flew to the roofs. Luckily the old station was deserted , because hundreds of turkeys trying to all roost on those old shingle roofs started caving in the rafters. The old barn crashed with a roar and more birds crowded the Station house. Henry told Helen that it would be much safer staying in the wagon overnight. He hoped that he wouldn't lose too many birds under the falling timbers.

Luckily, the remaining structures held up and the birds settled down.

Morning brought light to the turkey destruction of the night before. The old barn had no roof left and the walls were leaning inward. If any birds were killed in the evening crash, there was no evidence of it. Moving north along the river, they passed a few farms and sold thirty four birds for breeding stock. Henry was not gonna cut his price and even upped it to eight dollars for the big Tom's. Helen became the money holder and banker for all sales. This venture was starting to look better all the time! The river was wide and flat for miles ahead and Henry wanted to get across before they got into rough swift water.

That old wagon wouldn't take too much of a beating and it contained all of their corn feed and supplies. Unfortunately, the river got worse the further north they traveled! Henry was wishing that he had crossed further down stream and he knew that he had to cross before they hit the west river bank and high Sierra slopes. He was not familiar with this part of the trail and things were looking worse all the time. To turn around and go back ten miles to a crossing, would cost them another day. His only hope was; the roadway was good and appeared to be well travelled. He pushed ahead , hoping there might be a low crossing ahead. Suddenly the boys and Pedro stopped up ahead!

Henry was riding the Mustang and rode up to see what stopped the parade! There crossing the river was a beautiful sight for Henry! It was the

Carson Valley Covered Bridge! A good hundred feet long, recently built and perfect for parading across a couple thousand turkeys ,but it was a Toll Bridge! The keeper, a big surly unkempt bearded man; had stopped the boys and was completely surrounded by hundreds of turkeys. He was attempting to kick the birds away and getting madder all the time. He yelled at Henry, "Get these damned birds off this bridge!" Henry said , " I will! I will!!, What's the fee for crossing?" Rufus the Bridge tender said," One dollar per animal and two for the wagon! It'll be fifty for the turkeys!" Henry said, "Mister that's highway robbery! I'll pay for the animals and wagon, but the turkeys don't need your bridge, they'll fly across!" The bearded one answered, "Look , you either pay for the whole bunch or none of you go across!" Then he yelled, " Get that Jackass off that bridge!!"

The boys and Pedro were already half way across and the birds were milling around the entrance when Mister Nasty Rufus started running across to grab Pedro and drag him back! Pedro, with a little help from the boys; took off running! Rudy was yelling to the boys in Spanish and as soon as they hit the roadway on the other side , they gave a few yelps and started throwing out corn! That whole hoard of turkeys took off running across that hooded bridge filling the air and deck with hundreds of birds flying and crowding to get to the feed on the other side! Ol' Mister Nasty turned around yelling and was met , downed and trampled by what Helen later stated was nineteen hundred and fifty six stampeding turkeys!! Henry then rode up to what he referred to later as the "Turkey Basted Toll Bridge Road Agent"! He handed this fuming angry and dirty foul mouthed operator, his six dollars in fees! Helen, Rudy and the dogs were already headed down the road! Carson City, get ready for a real gaggle of gobblers!!

One more days drive and the turkeys were in the lower Carson ranches and Helen was filling her money box. They had camped in a local grove of trees near the river and put up sale signs for turkeys! The Comstock Mines were booming and prices were high every where! Most buyers were looking for roast turkey, but a number of the ranchers were wanting to get breeders. All of the larger Tom's sold for $8 dollars and everything else was $5 dollars. Folk's hearing of the turkey herd, were driving in from outside town to buy . It was an exciting time for everyone. Henry kept a rifle handy because, Stage holdup's were fairly common and the lawlessness around Carson was a big concern. Helen was fearful of some of the rough looking mining element and deposited all of their money in the local Citizens Bank. It wouldn't do to lose everything at the end of a Great Turkey Drive!

No sooner said than here comes Ol' Nasty Rufus from the bridge! He is accompanied by two other well dressed and important looking men. Rufus said , " Here they are Marshall, the thieving Toll runners that they cheated me outta $50 dollars !" The Marshall said, " Folk's I'm Territorial Marshall, Wayne Goslin . You have been charged with running Toll with thousands of turkeys and in this town, that's a jailing and fine offence ! Judge Brisneer here, owns the bridge!" Henry said , " Marshall and you too, Judge! It was a hold-up! The Toll Keeper here asking six dollars for a wagon and two kids on a burro! Then he runs across the bridge leading my turkeys over. I had planned on flying them across." The Marshall said, " Is this true Rufus? And where are the thousands of turkeys you claim stampeded over you? There's only about a dozen in the cages over there!"

Rufus looked around and "lo and behold" there were no thousands of turkeys. He cursed, strongly insisting that Henry was hiding the turkeys! The Marshall said, "Judge, it sounds to me like Rufus is being a little high handed and he may be drinking a little too much!' The Judge agreed, saying; " I'm gonna post signs at the Bridge. That way there won't be any question on charges. I may have to get a new Tollman! Thousands of turkeys? Stampeding and trampling you! I wonder, what had you been drinking?"

Another day , and Henry told Helen, " We're out of feed!" Helen told Henry, " We're out of turkeys!" Rudy said , " We're out of business!" Henry said, " No Rudy, its time for us to get in business together and go find that Ranch. I don't know how long this Mining Boom will go on, but we need to go find some beef to sell these miners! We've got a house to build and a Ranch to begin. The San Simon Valley is That-a -way!!

THE END

Epilogue: In early America, the herding and transport of Ducks and Turkeys was a common practice. Some of these drives covered hundreds of miles and always involved hundreds of birds. Many incidents of strange turkey behavior resulted in unusual adventures. One such involved a turkey herding that covered a full year transporting a herd of breeders from New Mexico to California.

Every year the turkey breeders of the New England states , walked thousands to the markets in New York City. This was a very common practice until the automobile and truck provided a better and faster transport. The story "Stampede of the Gobblers" is a fictionalized version of the original Henry Hooker Turkey Walk from Placerville to Carson City conducted in the early 1860's. Henry took his turkey fortune and invested it in building the beautiful Santa Bonita Ranch in the San Simon Valley of southeastern Arizona.